Remedios

Remedios

a novel by
Deborah Clearman

LIBRARY OF CONGRESS CATALOGING-IN-PUBLICATION DATA

Remedios
Authored by Deborah Clearman

ISBN: 978-1-7343835-0-8
LCCN: 2020935293

For E.B.F.M.

1

2012

THE RAINY SEASON, which had arrived like clockwork in Remedios since time immemorial, was late. Almost June, and haze and clouds hung oppressively in the sky but were unproductive—like Braxton Hicks contractions during pregnancy (Don Fernando, as a father of four, knew something about labor), or like a dry cough. Heat rose to epic proportions in Don Fernando's office at the university, causing even the insects that bludgeoned their way through his open window to circle dizzily and lie, prostrate and panting, on his desk.

It was hardly surprising. The climate was changing (everyone knew that), causing the great nations of the temperate zones to wrangle, create protocols, accuse each other of malfeasance and greed, miss treaty deadlines, etc. etc., everything except curb their appetites for comfort. Who could blame them? Don Fernando himself, sweat patches staining his formerly crisp short-sleeved polyester shirt by early afternoon, would have welcomed an air conditioner, if it were obtainable and affordable in the provincial capital Huehuetenango. However, those who were born in small countries in tropical latitudes had to resign themselves to hot tempers, rapid corruption of the flesh, and ronrones—the thumb-sized flying beetles that swarmed in streetlights and committed wanton, wholesale suicide against sidewalks, walls, tables, whatever surfaces their crazed, armor-encrusted primitive bodies found. They crunched under your feet, fell into your soup, dashed into your forehead—evolution's mistake. Those that survived their springtime awakening burrowed into the ground to become the farmers' scourge.

Farmers' scourge? Worry over the Rattlesnake was addling his brain with such high-flown language, because really, after the last student left his office—a pretty girl with a mind like cement—and Don Fernando unbuttoned one more button of his shirt, the heat was not apocalyptic, not when he thought back over his forty-eight years on the planet. Hot days were normal this time of year. So why did he feel so oppressed? And what had he been thinking when he took that loan, an avowed Marxist showing off like the bourgeoisie? Just as he finished putting away his papers his door opened again to admit a visitor.

It took Fernando a moment to place him. His wild mop of curly hair had been trimmed to a close cap, starting to gray, but his eyebrows still crawled like fat black caterpillars above small, hard eyes. Scrawny as a youth, always hungry as Fernando recalled, he'd filled out, but not the way Fernando had, as soft and rounded as a comfortable armchair, but with wide shoulders and a broad chest that bulged under a well-cut, light blazer. "Memo!" Fernando exclaimed. "Memo Golindo, by God. You just about gave me a heart attack. When did you get into town?"

"You remember me. I thought you might not." His thin lips stretched into an uneasy smile. "I've just come from the bus terminal, actually."

Fernando came around his desk, took the small suitcase out of Memo's hand with his left, so that he could shake with his right, a series of enthusiastic pumps. "Hombre! How long has it been since we horsed around in Father Reilly's math class? Thirty years?"

"About that."

"Where are you staying? I was just about to go home for lunch. Join me. We'll catch up." It was an impulse, the most natural of impulses, because hospitality was second nature to Fernando. Whatever misgivings he might have had, based on a quick appraisal of his old chum's appearance coupled with vague rumors over the years, gave way to small stirrings of excitement. Striding across the courtyard to the line of parked cars, carrying Memo's suitcase in one hand, Fernando pulled out his phone and called his wife. "We're having a guest for lunch. Set an extra place." Sandra would provide; she was practiced at last minute invitations.

The midday traffic between the metropolis of Huehuetenango and its smaller and older satellite Remedios was insane as always. Fernando steered his lumbering SUV past slow-moving, fume-spewing buses and pickups, dodged potholes, braked for axle-destroying speed bumps. "Can you believe this?" he asked Memo, who sat quietly peering out through the dark glass of the car windows.

"Little Huehue has grown up," Memo said dryly.

"Fucking politicians," Fernando said. "They've been arguing for years about a ring road. It's not going to happen until the mayor of the day makes a bundle off it." He hoped Memo was impressed by his late-model Toyota. Last time he'd seen Memo they'd been kids hitching rides, sneaking into the movies to smoke pilfered cigarettes in the balcony and throw the glowing butts over the edge, into the audience below. "What have you been up to? I heard you were in the special forces." He didn't want to say the name Kaibil, because frankly, the business of biting the heads off live chickens, not to mention the massacres of innocent civilians, repulsed him. In his side vision he saw Memo swivel his head toward him without moving his shoulders. He had removed the blazer and laid it across the back seat when they got into the car, but there were no sweat stains on his black polo shirt. His biceps confirmed Fernando's initial impression. His hands rested lightly on his thighs.

"Me? I had a desk job," Memo said. "Anyway, I've been out of the army a long time. Working abroad."

"Well, you've stayed in shape." He decided not to ask him about his work abroad. Rather, he balanced Memo's silence with his chatter, pointing out landmarks along the route and their associated dramas, new business ventures, old families fallen to ruin, until he pulled up the narrow cobbled street and stopped in front of his house. It was a long, single-story stucco façade in a row of similar façades, punctuated by narrow doors and iron-work grilled windows, on its right solid metal double gates barely wide enough to admit a car. He honked for the servant girl.

"Remember the old place, Memo?"

La Tona swung the gates open and Fernando maneuvered the big car up the short driveway and parked in the carport. Leaving the suitcase in the car, he led Memo through the courtyard garden, noting with satisfaction that it was looking lush, the hibiscus and gladiolas a symphony of red and gold. He casually pointed out the fine second-story brick addition he'd just built onto the interior wing of the house for his growing family. Accomplishment, not hubris after all. "Lots of changes since my grandfather's day. I'll take you upstairs after lunch. There's a view of all Remedios."

The Chihuahua bounded toward them yapping furiously and attempted to hump Memo's ankle. Fernando yelled, "Get lost, Mozart!" but before he could scoop the dog up, Memo thrust it away with a convulsive kick. Fernando thought once again of the chicken heads. But Mozart was unharmed, trotted off unperturbed and chipper as ever, and Lord knows Fernando had been ready to strangle the irrepressible little animal often enough himself. His eleven-year-old daughter Leti emerged from the kitchen to announce that lunch was served.

The dining room in the old part of the house, with its thick walls and high ceilings, stayed cool even in the afternoon heat. They kept the electric light off, and daylight filtered in through the window from the courtyard. The dark mahogany furniture of his grandparents—the breakfront, the long table, the stiff high-backed chairs—and the murky religious paintings stood sentry in the gloom, as if the ghost of his grandfather still lingered to reprimand bad boys. In defiance of the ghost, Fernando took his accustomed seat at the head of the table, put Memo on his right, and as the family filed in and sat in their places he poured red wine into Memo's glass. "I brought a whole case of this back from Italy," he said. He too was a man of the world, not just a small town player who'd never left home, he wanted Memo to know. "To springtime in Roma," he toasted. "*Bellissimo.*"

"Never been there," Memo said. "I was in Israel."

"Some good wines there, too, I hear. It's the Mediterranean climate that counts."

"Mmmm. Perhaps. I didn't have time to sample them. I was...working."

"Too bad! My brother, Elías, has been to Israel. Great wines, great oranges, great beaches, eh Elías?" Elías, the doughy-looking man to Memo's right, nodded.

"You remember Memo, soccer star of San Francisco Javier!" Fernando said to him, and to the tall thin brother Edgar. Both much older, Edgar had been off teaching in the mountains and Elías at university when Memo had frequented the house in Remedios. Fernando grew more ebullient with each glass of wine, and kept filling Memo's glass. Sandra moved back and forth between the dining room and the kitchen with easy grace, bringing in dishes of food, directing the children to help. The two middle children, Leti and Walter, sat at the far end of the table, elbowing each other until their mother told them to stop. The toddler was napping and Félix, in high school in Huehue, didn't come home for lunch. Fernando as host and lord of the manor steered the table talk onward. "So, what's the news of the day? You tell us, Edgar. You're always watching the telly."

"Only this," the thin brother said, using a tortilla to wipe up the sauce from his plate. Probably his sixth or seventh tortilla; Edgar could eat and eat and never get fat, a source of annoyance to his plumper brothers. "The president wants out of the drug war. Fíjese! He's calling on Central American leaders to legalize drugs. To be discussed at the big summit next month." He chuckled. "That will get some attention."

"Ridiculous!" Sandra exclaimed, frowning at her broth-er-in-law. "Is this how we safeguard our children?" She was perhaps more concerned with appropriate topics of conver-sation in their presence than the specter of their drug use.

"Where's his iron fist?" Elías referred to the emblem of the president's party. "And his promise to rid Guatemala of drug lords?"

"Every Guatemalan president makes and breaks that promise. You thought this one would be different just because he was a general?" Fernando didn't say *genocidal general* as he normally would have, not with Memo sitting at his side.

"That's just his point," Edgar said. "To put the drug lords out of business. Portugal has tried it, with great success so they say."

"Hah!" This from Elías. "The narcos have plenty of other businesses—protection, kidnapping, assassination. Right, Memo? You've been living in Mexico. Look what happened there when the government went against the cartels."

"I stay away from politics," Memo said. "For my health."

"No kidding!" Fernando said. "Politics in Guatemala is an unhealthy game. Have more fish. A little more salad? More tortillas!" It was time to turn the conversation, which had wandered into dangerous territory. He wanted to fill Memo up with his wife's good cooking, his good cheer, his beautiful family—Sandra, who had once been his student, was still dark-haired and whippet-thin after four children; Walter and Leti looking dapper in their school uniforms and showing their manners—and let whatever it was that Memo had on his mind rise to the surface. Because surely, something was on his mind, to appear without warning after thirty years of silence.

"The kids have to get back to school," Sandra said when coffee and dessert had been served and only crumbs remained. "Memo, so nice to have met you." She looked to the children and there was a chorus of "Gracias, buen provecho" around the table as Leti and Walter cleared their places. Elías also left, to go back to his store, a small room in the front of the house with a separate entrance onto the street, where he sold beer, liquor, and soft drinks. Sandra stood to follow the children.

Memo touched his lips with his paper napkin. "Delicious meal, Doña Sandra. Congratulations, Nando, on achieving such domestic fulfillment, something that's sadly lacking in my life."

Fernando used this cue to leap up and grab a bottle and more glasses from the sideboard. "A little brandy, for old time's sake, Memo. It's never too late," he added, now that the room was clear of women and children, "for a young and handsome guy like you."

Memo didn't even smile at the compliment. He leaned back in his chair and stared into his brandy snifter. Then he raised his eyes to Fernando. "I'm retiring. Work has been… stressful lately. I'm looking for a quiet, secluded place. To work on my memoirs. You know, I don't have family in Huehuetenango any more."

"I heard. Condolences on the loss of your mother. A good woman, Doña Tina."

"Thank you. Would you know of someplace? I can pay rent, of course."

So there it was: the purpose of the visit. Fernando had been waiting for it, with dread and anticipation. Hoping it wouldn't be too risky (he was a family man after all, and had to put the well-being of his wife and children first), but that it might help him get out of a sticky situation. Memo wanted to hide out. Who didn't these days? What with small government planes circling every morning at daybreak searching for marijuana or poppy fields hidden in the pinewoods or milpas, armed assaults on buses on the rise, extortionists ever more brazen, everyone was on edge. But carrying on, as chapines did, because violence was nothing new to Guatemala. It took a clever man to prosper and keep his family safe these days. Fernando was a clever man. "I have the perfect spot for you. On family property, just out of town, four kilometers from here—Edgar walks there all the time, don't you?" Edgar, who had moved to the chair to Memo's right, shrugged.

"A charming spot, Sapoclok," Fernando continued. "A valley at the foot of the mountains, nothing in it but some cornfields and a couple of country houses. The whole thing belonged to our great grandfather, and it's been divided into inheritances, so there are cousins out there de vez en cuando. At the head of the valley is our eldest brother's house, we call it the Pink House, but he's never there, he lives in Mexico. An excellent retreat, don't you think, Edgar?"

Edgar agreed that it would be convenient to have someone staying in the house, to discourage the burglars that were a constant problem. Even with the Doberman they kept on the premises, thieves had managed to break in just last month and make off with an old set of cookware they kept for weekend barbecues.

"You can see it from the roof deck. Come along for the house tour," Fernando said, rising from the table. The servant girl Tona had cleared the last of the dishes. Edgar excused himself to go run an errand in town, and Fernando led Memo up the grand staircase set with sparkling ceramic tile made to imitate wood parquet, and showed off the airy master bedroom with its shutters open to reveal a view of the face of the mountain range that towered five thousand feet over Remedios. "It gets better further up," he said. Passing a glass case with Sandra's collection of porcelain bird figurines and open doorways on two modern bathrooms of which he was intensely proud, they continued up the stairs to the roof door, which like all the woodwork in the addition was naturally golden-toned and gleaming with varnish.

The door opened onto a flat roof edged by a low brick wall. Several large-leafed plants grew in big pots, but as yet there was no other furnishing on the roof, although Fernando had plans. Certainly there were no clotheslines, so typical of rooftops; they were downstairs in the back courtyard of the house where the laundry sink and old wood stove were. Up here nothing obstructed the view of the Cuchumatanes shimmering in the afternoon heat, rising to the altiplano, a flock of birds circling high overhead, and the town clustered below. Behind Fernando's house, where in his grandfather's time there had been open fields and orchards, houses abutted each other in every available space. Fernando pointed out the houses of his brothers, sisters, uncles, and cousins until Memo commented, "The Granados family seems to be overpopulating the town."

Fernando laughed. "Not any more. I'm stopping at four. And three of my brothers have no kids at all. The ones who live here with me."

"It's good to have family around." He said nothing more, and Fernando didn't ask about his younger siblings. As he recalled, there had been a lot of them, and they'd been very poor. Only Memo, the eldest, had gone to high school, and he'd been on scholarship.

The birds circled lower, seemingly focused on a point nearby. The clock in the town square struck four. "I have to be getting back for my evening classes soon," Fernando said. "You'll stay here tonight. My brother Luis is in Mexico; you can use his room. Tomorrow Sandra will take you out and get you settled into the Pink House. There's Sapoclok, behind that ridge."

He pointed to the left of the clock tower and double domes of the church, just visible above the trees of the square, to a pine-covered hill opposite the mountain range, in the distance beyond the town.

"It looks very peaceful." As if to emphasize tranquility, the birds wheeling overhead cooed.

"They're looking for their dinner," Fernando explained. "My wife feeds the pigeons."

The flock turned in unison, flew up, then dipped down again in a tightening circle.

"Remember how we used to shoot at them with slingshots, when we were kids?" Fernando asked.

Memo smiled, drew a small black contraption out of his pocket, and unfolded it. A molded handle, a steel fork, a yellow tubular sling, it looked like an updated version of the twig and rubber band.

"I don't believe it! You've got one," Fernando said, feeling his youthful devil kicking in. He looked around the rooftop for ammunition, and spied the gravel lining the planters. He picked up a pebble and offered it to Memo, who refused it. Instead, he handed Fernando the sling saying, "You first."

Fernando laughed. "OK!" He fitted the pebble into the sling, and stared up into the sky. The pigeons rose and fell, circling closer. It had been a long time since he'd done this. He picked one bird, a dark charcoal, almost black one, and tried to draw a bead onto it, following its movements with his arms poised to shoot. The birds seemed oblivious to the threat and kept wheeling lower. He felt his heart race, let fly the pebble, and missed.

"Oh well! I guess I need some practice." He felt strangely disappointed as he handed the sling back to Memo.

Memo picked up a pebble and looked up at the birds. They seemed ready to alight at any moment. "The white one," he said. With a movement so swift Fernando couldn't follow it, he raised the slingshot, released the pebble, and the white dove dropped to the rooftop and lay still. Fernando couldn't tell if it was dead or just stunned. Memo picked it up by the head and swung it sharply to break its neck.

"Not bad!" Fernando congratulated him. "You'll never go hungry in the jungle."

Memo put the little weapon back in his pocket and grunted. "Shall we give it to the servant girl to take home for her supper?"

—

Fernando was still thinking about Memo, his miraculous reappearance right at this moment, as though he'd been sent by a Higher Power (if there was one), when he got back to the university. He was distracted, not up to lecturing, so he decided a class discussion was in order. Let the students do the work tonight. "Money is the root of all evil," he began, addressing his class in introductory political theory, getting things off the ground with a bang. "Is that what Marx is telling us?" They'd been reading *Das Kapital.*

There had been a time when Fernando had agreed with Marx, that profit represented the portion of value *improperly appropriated*—i.e. stolen—by capital owners instead of accruing to workers who, as sole producers of goods from scratch to end, should by rights benefit from all or at least most (por Jesucristo!), of the income. That had been back when men like Fidel and Ché were the standard bearers. To this day he supported Evo, even through the gasolinazo debacle. But Chávez stuck in his craw.

Marielena, who always sat in the front row and always participated in class, raised her hand. "It's 'Love of money is the root of all evil,'" she corrected him. "Paul's first epistle to Timothy 6:10."

An Evangelical of course, Fernando thought, amused. She would know her New Testament chapter and verse. But it wasn't love of money that had gotten him into his current jam. It was love of family, wanting his children to have rooms of their own and not have to sleep with their parents and uncles snoring beside them. His problems had reached critical proportions when he had borrowed money from the Rattlesnake. Everyone knew what happened when you didn't make the payments. But what could Fernando do after the bank turned him down?

"Would Marx have agreed?" he asked the rest of the class. "By removing profit and loss as motivators, people are naturally good?"

Look at Cuba, sending its doctors to help the poor all over Latin America.

His students hotly debated the pros and cons of state ownership.

"Makes people lazy!"

"Government is corrupt!"

"Business is corrupt!"

"Marx said if you give capitalism enough rope, it will hang itself," Jorge the class Communist said. "Look around. Bank bailouts, Euro zone coming apart, te digo, you're seeing the beginning of the end."

Listening to them made Fernando proud. His seminar style of teaching unlocked minds, instead of killing them with the dry lectures he'd suffered through in university. However, when the end of the school year came in October, he would give the same grueling exams—long essay questions requiring factually correct answers on every topic covered in the course—that were the staple of his education. Some things—like the ronrones buzzing in from the night outside his classroom window, attracted by the beacon of florescent light—never changed.

2

MEMO SAT SHOTGUN AGAIN, this time with Sandra at the wheel of the Toyota SUV. They'd traded cars this morning, Fernando taking her small sedan to the university because Sandra needed four-wheel drive to get out to Sapoclok. Memo watched the route they took, noting where they turned off the main road out of Remedios onto a dirt road that climbed up a ridge, past a knot of houses and a miniature church. He wanted to know how to get in and out of this place on his own if he had to. He also watched Sandra. He could do that—watch two things at once—and keep his mind focused on both things simultaneously. It amazed him how few people had the mental discipline to pull this off. He admired her handling of the car over the ruts and potholes. She was a slender, petite thing, but under her delicate veneer Memo sensed the strength of a thoroughbred. She ran a household of four men and four children, servants and pets and constant visitors, and made it look easy. Memo liked powerful women.

"Hang on," she said. They'd passed the last house, reached the top of the hill, and now the road dove down to the right. Memo noted with satisfaction that it was still wide enough to accommodate a decent sized truck. That was important for his purposes. "We have to cross the river," she said when they reached the edge of a broad, flat area of rock and gravel threaded through with a tangled maze of streams. "It's easy this time of year."

"Are there times when it's impassable?" he asked.

"After a heavy rain. But there's another way out on the other side, just a track, and roundabout, but it works." She revved the motor carefully and they plunged into the stream with momentum to carry them through to the other side. They crossed the dry gravel bed, weaving through boulders, fording two more streams, Sandra showing her expertise, until they climbed the opposite shore, where they picked up a dirt road that led to a metal gate. Sandra stopped the car, got out, unlocked a padlock on the gate, and swung it open. "Beyond this, all the land belongs to the family," she said when she was back behind the wheel.

"A little bit of paradise," Memo said, looking out over plowed fields, planted and waiting for rain, protected on the opposite side by a low ridge of pines. A white house sat in the center of the valley, down a long drive on their right.

"It could be," Sandra said. "But the family fights over water rights and every inch of land. My husband isn't speaking to the cousin who owns that house."

"Typical of paradise," Memo said. "There are always problems."

They drove alongside the dry river to the top of the gentle valley, where the pine ridge on the right curved to meet them. Here Sandra parked beside a chain link fence topped in barbed wire surrounding a house and an unkempt garden. The grass was long, unpruned bushes sent out rangy sprays of bug-eaten roses, a bougainvillea climbed a tree half strangled in its magenta blossoms, and orange trees were heavy with unharvested fruit. The house competed with the riotous garden—a one-story L-shaped building painted flamingo pink. Turquoise posts held up the veranda that ran the length of the house. Memo thought about how easy it would be to pick out in satellite view. At least the roof was a sedate terra cotta tile. A dog charged toward them barking and leapt at the fence. The Doberman.

"Quiet, Telegram," Sandra told it, sticking her fingers through the chain link to fondle the dog's ear. Standing on its hind legs, it wagged its tail eagerly. "He's really a sweetheart," Sandra said. Memo followed her through the gate carrying his suitcase and a bag of groceries. While she unlocked the doors to the house he looked beyond the garden, to an orchard of gnarled avocado trees and the fields that stretched to the foot of the valley. In the distance he could see mountains and the hazy cone of a volcano. Now that Telegram had stopped barking, the quiet was profound.

"The furniture isn't much," Sandra said, leading him through a series of rooms that opened onto each other. Dull, blocky sofas, narrow beds promising little comfort, it had the look of a place that had been equipped with cast-offs. An empty Scotch bottle and dusty glasses testified to weekend revelries. The walls of the house were a kaleidoscope. From the soft gold living room they passed through lime green, pale lilac, and arrived at a robin's egg blue bedroom. High windows let in light, but their glass was milky so Memo couldn't see out. The house turned all of his attention inward, on itself and its lavish paint. The windows facing the property line were barred with an ornate black grillwork.

"How did the burglars get in?" Memo asked.

"They broke the lock on the door, after giving Telegram a big bone to chew on. We found the bone and the dog with a fat belly. Who knows what else they gave him." The blue room contained a double bed, a wooden desk and chair, and a mahogany wardrobe. The room of choice. Sandra took the spread off the bed and began making it up with sheets she'd brought with her. "Fernando and his brothers usually keep a gun here when we stay overnight. For protection. I hope you won't need it."

"Don't worry," Memo said. He wouldn't need it. Not wanting to stand idle while she worked, he put down his bags and moved to the opposite side of the bed from her. "Let me help." He picked up a corner of the sheet she was holding and pulled it taut between them. She startled and unaccountably blushed, as if she was unaccustomed to a man's taking on this task. Probably in her house it was considered women's work.

"I guess in the army you learned to make your own bed," she said, recovering her composure. "My husband tells me you were a dangerous man." She smiled, narrowing her eyes, tilting her head back as if to look down on him.

"Are you afraid of me?"

"Oh no!" She laughed and tossed her long dark hair. Memo wondered if she were afraid of anything. Together they tucked the bottom sheet around the mattress. Then Sandra passed an edge of the top sheet to him and they spread it on the bed, smoothing it, patting it into place. Watching Sandra's slender fingers gliding across the bed, her olive skin contrasting against the white of the sheet, Memo felt a shiver cross his flesh. They moved in opposition to each other, smoothing and tucking, then doubling the top edge back. Sandra picked up a pillow and tossed it across the bed to him. She picked up the other and held it in her teeth as she slid it into the pillowcase. Memo had a strong feeling that she wanted him to kiss her. The idea intrigued him, but he decided to let her wait.

"Very good," she said. "You can always get a job in a fine hotel. Come on. Let me show you the bathroom and kitchen." She swept out onto the veranda and talked with her back to him. "La Tona lives just up the road, in a house Fernando's father gave her. She comes by every day to feed Telegram. She'll bring your tortillas to you in the morning on her way to work."

The dining room and kitchen were in the L, with the kitchen on the end, its window overlooking the valley. It had the usual cinderblock wood stove for cooking as well as a propane cook top and small refrigerator which Sandra loaded with the supplies they'd bought in the market that morning to add to the staples kept in the cabinet—fresh eggs, oranges, limes, onions, chilies, some linked sausages that Memo had chosen. "The sink is out back." Sandra opened the kitchen door opposite the veranda and went outside, carrying a coffee pot that Memo watched her fill from the faucet at the sink. Beyond the sink, there was another gate in the fence encircling the property, padlocked shut. A small shed outside the fence was also padlocked.

"Very comfortable. Everything I need," Memo said when she came back in.

"I just have time for a cup of coffee, then I have to go get the kids from school." She lit the propane stove and put the pot on. They waited for the water to boil. "Where are you from?" she asked. The question could have been casual, to fill the time. "My husband says you're Remediosino, but…I don't think so."

Memo gave her the smallest smile he had. "No? You don't think I look local?" He knew she was talking about his curly hair, his height, subtle clues that made him look foreign. "My mother was from Remedios. She was poor, ran away from home at fourteen, went to the capital to work as a maid."

That was the official story. Memo knew the real story, he had pieced it together: hunger, desperation, the pimp who picked her up off the street in Guatemala City and gave her a home and a job. Until she met the curly-haired truck driver from the east who got her out of there. Took her home to his mamá's house up against the border of El Salvador, where she found she had another job—cooking and cleaning for her mother-in-law and making babies.

"My father died when I was thirteen," Memo said. "My mother brought us back to Remedios." That was also the official version. He didn't know if his father had died, but he was out of Memo's life. "That's where I'm from, little town in the east, then back here, my mother still dirt poor, now with five kids. She thought her family would help her out, but . . ." Memo shrugged. "What could they do?"

Sandra poured boiling water into two mugs and spooned in instant coffee. "Sugar?" she asked.

"Black," he said. And she put the mug in front of him and sat down across from him at the small kitchen table.

"That's when you met Fernando."

"In school. On the soccer field. Soccer is what got me the scholarship to go to high school."

"Fernando says in addition to soccer, you were a smart kid."

"Does he?" Memo arched his furry eyebrows at Sandra. "Your husband seems to be my biggest fan."

Sandra stared down at the table between them with pursed lips. "Everything in this house is covered with dust. I don't know what Fernando was thinking, inviting you here. It needs a good cleaning."

"Don't worry." This was a favorite expression of Memo's. He liked the power that it had to create anxiety when there was none, or heighten it when there was. "I'll take care of it. I like to sweep. And wash up." He stood up and took her empty coffee mug with his own outside and left them in the sink, then walked with her back to where her car was parked out front. The dog trotted along with them.

"Take Telegram with you if you go for walks," Sandra said.

"For protection?"

"For company. It's lonely out here." She shuddered. "You're going to be very bored. I wish we at least had a TV for you."

"You've been very generous," Memo said with a look that made her blush again.

He watched her drive away. There goes a strange one, he thought. Back inside, he unpacked his bag, hanging his shirts and pants in the wardrobe. He folded sweaters and socks into drawers and slid his chanate—the M4 Carbine with grenade launcher—into a drawer under a towel. He changed into jeans and hiking shoes, transferring his pistol into his waistband, and went outside to the back gate behind the kitchen. Under the watchful eyes of Telegram, he tried the ring of keys Sandra had given him until he opened the padlock. He let the dog come with him, and locked the gate behind himself.

With Telegram running on ahead, he climbed up the ridge in back of the house, on a footpath through widely spaced pines. There was little underbrush, just needles on the ground, spicing the air with their scent. The midday sun was scorching, and even in the shade it was hot. Probably he should have waited until later to get the lay of the land, but he was impatient. He wasn't surprised that there was a path. Fernando had told him the local peasants went in there to graze their sheep and steal firewood. The path led him to the top of the ridge, then it plunged down through thickets of live oaks, alders, and willows into a deep ravine. He stopped at the top to survey the distant hills and the valley of Sapoclok spread out below. The only houses visible were the Pink House and the cousin's, secluded and remote, ideal for hidden activity. He took a tiny digital camera out of his pocket and snapped a few photos.

3

1978

THE TALL KID WITH THE wild mop of curly hair was all over the field, everywhere the ball was. Fernando had never seen him before in the pickup games they played every Sunday afternoon. Playing offense for the Rojos, the kid wove down field like an eel, passing the ball to Rodrigo, slithering inside the Azules' defense to receive it again inside the six-yard box and drive in a low-angle shot that was too fast and close for the goalie to protect. After that, playing midfield, Nando tried to stay on top of him, scrambling to grab the ball. But the kid was crafty as well as fast. Dribbling toward Nando he managed to kick the ball between Nando's feet, whip around him, pick it up on the other side and send it toward the goal in a high shot at the upper-right 90 that hit the crossbeam but bounced away without touching twine.

The game held at 1-0 and the players danced up and down the field, Nando sticking to the new guy, getting separated from him by attackers from the Rojos, sometimes by his own defense, then finding him again, the kid always going for the ball like he and it were two asteroids meeting in outer space, destined to cross paths, nothing else out there but emptiness.

Finally Nando managed to take control, kicking the ball out from between the new guy's feet and passing it on to the

Azules' striker who fired it in for a goal. Five minutes left to play and they were tied. The new kid raced toward the Azules' goal with a clump of players surrounding him like a swarm of bees. The Rojos kicked off. Nando ran to meet the ball, his heart pounding, feeling his pulse in his forehead, his cleats churning the dirt, the ball bounding toward him in a high arc, the players running circles to position themselves, the new kid breaking free of the pack, heading straight toward Nando. Before he could alter his course, or wonder at his opponent's suicidal attack, or throw out his arms to defend himself, they crashed. Nando hit the dirt; the new kid sprawled on top of him. The ball bounced out of bounds and the game ended.

Nando pushed off his opponent and sat up, shook his head getting his wind back, then turned to the new kid. He lay stretched out on his back, staring up at the sky, mouth and eyes wide open, his back arched, his arms thrown out. He was gasping for breath. His face was streaked with dirt. His black hair stuck out in corkscrew curls, like the cartoon character who had stuck his finger in a socket. His thick black eyebrows made exclamation points across his face.

"Are you OK?" Nando asked.

The kid rolled his head from side to side, muscles standing out on his skinny neck. He reached his hands behind his head to haul himself up to sitting. Nando stood up and held out his hand to grasp his opponent's and raise him to his feet. The kid leaned over and brushed the dirt from his knees and shiny red shorts. "Yeah," he said.

The players gathered around them. Nando said to the new kid, "You want to go get a Coke?"

That was how Fernando met Memo. That first afternoon, after the soccer game, the two boys walked from the field the few blocks to Nando's house, where the maid María, who was the mother of Antonia who would be Don Fernando's servant girl thirty years later, let them in and brought out two small bottles of cold Coke to the table in the patio, in the shade of the veranda. Roses were blooming in the courtyard, and a sweet smell hung in the air. The boys, sweaty and dirty, sucked the Cokes down and Nando peppered Memo with questions. When had he gotten to town? Last month. Where was he from? Eastern Guatemala, by way of a year in the capital. Where was he in school? Right now—nowhere. He was working as a shoeshine to help support his younger siblings, on account of his father wasn't around.

"Mine isn't around much either," Nando said. "He teaches school in a little town up in the mountains. Sometimes he comes home weekends." He lowered his voice and leaned across the table closer to Memo. "He hasn't been home in six months. He's with some woman. Money's tight with us too. My mother makes candies and sells them in the market."

The kitchen door opened, letting out more of the sweet smell, which hadn't been coming from the roses after all, and Nando's mother, a stout woman with a tired face and heavy dark hair in a low bun, came toward them wiping her hands on a flowered apron. "Fernando, look at you!" she said, after introductions. "Take a shower, both of you, right now."

Memo seemed unfamiliar with the working of the shower, and Nando guessed he was used to bathing in a bucket. But he had a change of clothes in his soccer bag that were an improvement on his uniform, which he confessed he'd borrowed.

"Give it to me," Nando said, taking the red shorts and shirt. "I'll get María to wash it, and you can give it back. Next week you're wearing blue."

They became best friends. After getting Memo to play for the Azules, Nando's next step was to have Father Reilly, the math teacher who also coached soccer, come out to Remedios and watch Memo play. So that by the end of the year, when his father had rejoined the family, taking a little of the strain off the budget, Fernando had secured a scholarship for Memo. They would enter high school in Huehue together.

Nando had always been such a good boy. The youngest of nine, he was protected by his older brothers and doted on by his sisters—the little prince. Memo offered him a chance to change his image. Memo was firstborn, poor, hardened by his year in the city and things that came before it. Just being around him gave Nando ideas. It was Nando's idea to steal the radio. He'd never stolen, but he knew Memo had. He didn't need a radio—they had radios and a TV in his house—but he figured Memo did. Memo lived in one room with his mother and younger siblings and had nothing but the school uniform and books that Father Reilly had gotten for him.

They hitched a ride into Huehue as they did most Saturdays. This would have been somewhere in that first year of high school, and they jumped off the back of the pickup before the driver could demand his payment, dashing around a corner out of sight, laughing when they heard the driver shouting after them, "Hijos de puta!"

Nando picked the store. It was called the Commissary for no good reason; there wasn't yet an army base in Huehue. It had aisles stacked with pots, pans, flowered china, baby toys, beach towels, screwdrivers, underwear, pretty much every household item in random order. Out of sight of the lone clerk at the cash register, Nando picked out the radio. It was a transistor radio, the size of a hardcover book, with shiny knobs and a discreet leather handle, to be carried like a miniature suitcase. Nando picked it up and tucked it under his arm. He signaled Memo with a quick nod and hung back. Memo sauntered up to the clerk at the front of the store. "Do you have any watches?" he asked.

The clerk eyed his ragged shirt and worn sneakers, his long curly hair, and frowned. "For you?" he asked.

"For my mother. It's her birthday."

"So you want a lady's watch." The clerk's tone said he didn't want to wait on Memo. "What price range?"

"Let's start with the most expensive. I love my mother." Memo was fifteen at this point, still tall for his age, and the shadow of a moustache already showed on his upper lip.

The clerk took a key out of his pocket, unlocked a black case, and drew out a slender gold watch, laying it on the counter where it sparkled with little rhinestones. Nando glided up the aisle toward Memo and the clerk, the radio shielded by his body from the clerk's gaze.

"How much?" Memo asked, picking up the watch and dangling it in front of the clerk like a fishing lure.

"Forty-nine quetzales." A vast sum.

Nando passed the clerk.

"Real gold?" Memo asked.

The clerk laughed. "Of course!" Even Memo knew he was lying.

Nando walked out the door.

"Do you have one in silver?" Memo asked.

The clerk put the gold watch back in the case and banged it shut. "Are you wasting my time, kid?"

"I told you, it's my mother's birthday. But maybe I'll go somewhere else to shop." He tossed his crazy hair back and started for the door. Nando was already out of sight. "Some-place where they want my money."

"You were good," Nando told him when they met up at the bus stop. "You think that guy is going to figure out he's missing a radio?"

"Maybe sometime next week," Memo said. They both cracked up.

That was Fernando's favorite memory, the one he liked to pull out like a DVD and play on the screen of his mind over the years, after Memo, and then his whole family, disappeared. But a lot of people disappeared in those years, including members of Fernando's family, the ones who didn't flee to Mexico and The North. The look on Memo's face when they were both laughing with such unrestrained joy, releasing the tension of the heist, Memo's eyes wide, his wild hair framing his face like a black halo, his skin smooth and gleaming with sweat, just the slightest dark fuzz on his upper lip and those black caterpillars arching over his wide eyes. Innocent: that's how he looked. That's how Fernando felt when he reviewed that memory. After he lost touch with Memo and made it unscathed through the years of the Violence, he never stole again, except for maybe claiming his brothers' purchases on his tax return once in a while, but that's not stealing. Still, he liked to remember that prank, dust it off and polish it up, over the years when he heard rumors about Memo.

Because there was another memory that he tried to keep buried. It was a girl that broke up their friendship. At seven-teen they'd been best pals for four years. But at seventeen it's always going to be about a girl. When Anita Carrillo showed up at the beginning of senior year, a buzz went around the hall-ways. Wasn't she off at some fancy boarding school? What was she doing back in Huehuetenango, a girl from her family, the richest family in town. The buzzing kept up, gathering steam until rumors spread that something had happened at her fancy school and her parents had snatched her out and brought her home where they could keep an eye on her.

Every boy in school had his eye on her. Her sassy haircut, her short skirts, her heels that somehow got away with being higher than the school permitted. It was at the first game of the season, with Anita sitting in the stands with a group of girlfriends, that Memo caught her eye. Naturally, Nando figured, since Memo was the soccer star of San Francisco Javier, not to mention tall, fast, and curly-haired. After the game she came up to him and said, "My parents are having a group of my friends over Sunday afternoon. Want to come?"

Memo, sweat still pouring off him from dashing down the field, said yes. Nando saw it from the sidelines.

Later Memo said to him, "What do I do? A girl like that. I don't have any clothes. I won't know how to behave in her house."

"Don't worry," Nando said. "I'll get you fixed up."

He took Memo shopping for a suit and tie, and sharp new shoes. "This isn't going to be a blue jeans party," he said. Even then, Nando was a little jealous. He wasn't sure if it was because he wanted Anita (who didn't?) or because he wanted Memo for himself. But he was determined to show his loyalty.

Jealousy nagged at Nando, at first just a little, like a scratchy sore throat that he could ignore. He would see Anita and Memo walking together in the halls and feel the scratch. After games now, Memo didn't go over to Nando's house; he and Anita went out, to the park, to movies, Nando didn't know any more where they went. Everyone assumed they were a couple.

Memo was invited to Anita's house every Sunday; it seemed that he'd learned pretty fast how to act around rich people. Nando's aggravation grew, the way a sore throat blooms into a full-body fever. The other guys at school moaned about losing out to Memo, but Nando wouldn't admit to envy. The fever grew, the jealousy he couldn't admit to without losing his pride, mixed with a sense of injustice. Who had befriended Memo? Who had gotten him onto the team, into the school, into the house of Carillo?

The worst of it was, there was nothing Nando could do about Memo's betrayal.

Or was there?

The idea first came to him on a day he was late getting home to Remedios for lunch. He'd hung out waiting for Memo to get out of class so that he could have a word with him, only to have Anita grab Memo's arm and steer him off saying, "No time for talk, boys. Memo, Mamá's waiting for us at home."

What! Going there on a weekday. Was he living at her house now?

In a bad mood, Nando slid into a chair at the opposite end of the dining table from his father, who scowled at him. "What kept you?" he demanded.

Nando's mother put a plate of rice and beans in front of him. His older sister Bela passed the basket of tortillas. "Sorry," Nando said. "I was doing extra work for Father Reilly, trying to improve my math grades."

"That's important, now more than ever," his brother Edgar, sitting next to Papá, said. What was Edgar doing here on a Tuesday? He was supposed to be up in Todos Santos, teaching. "You have to stay in school or you'll get drafted. University is the only safe place for a young man."

Memo was poor, Nando thought. If not for Nando, the army would be going after Memo. Now he had Anita looking out for him, but if not for Nando, that wouldn't have happened either.

"The university isn't safe either," Bela said. She was in her second year at San Carlos West. "Lucas García thinks all students are subversives."

Doña Teresa, Nando's mother, wrung her pudgy hands, hands worn out from making candies. "Where can anyone be safe these days?" Out of her nine children, six were either teachers or students.

"Stay home and keep quiet," Edgar said. "Pepe wants me to go to a meeting." Nando's oldest brother Pepe was a professor at San Carlos.

"What kind of meeting?" Doña Teresa asked.

"He says it's informal. At night, in a secret location."

"Insanity!" Nando's father, Don José, scowled more ferociously. "Meet with the guerrillas and you'll both be branded Communists. Don't go."

"The guerrillas have already come to Todos Santos," Edgar said. "I've heard them talk. They have good ideas."

"Like raising the Ché Guevara flag over the square? You call that a good idea?" Spit flew from Don José's lips. Nando knew his father's temper. "That's the idea that shut down your school. Your principal's no fool; he doesn't want to be there when the army marches in."

That explained why Edgar was home, and why his mother was so upset. María came out from the kitchen to see who wanted seconds. She loaded Nando's plate with more beans. Lately, since his father got sick and had to retire, they'd only had meat on weekends. Nando felt like he was always hungry. He grabbed more tortillas.

"Do we just let the generals like Lucas García get away with running the country?" Nando asked. "We just let him pick the next so-called president?" Nando wasn't political normally. But the meeting with the guerrillas intrigued him. He wondered if he could get Pepe to invite him. He wondered if he could get Memo to go.

It turned out, he could.

Pepe was delighted that his little brother was taking an interest in something other than soccer at last. "Just be a little smart," he warned Nando. "The meeting's at a safe house. Listen to me. If I say run, do it."

Memo couldn't resist. It would be like the heist at the Commissary—a little risk, a little danger, and they would run away laughing, Nando explained. "Just don't tell Anita," he said. If the house of Carillo found out that Memo had gone to a guerrilla meeting, they would end the relationship, the same way they had ended Anita's boarding school flirtation. Anita would be out of the picture. Nando planned for them to find out.

Edgar backed out, listening to their mother's pleas. Pepe reassured her that he could take care of Nando and Memo. Friday night the three of them hitched a ride to the safe house. Pepe had an old car, but didn't want to leave it parked near the meeting. It was at an isolated spot off the highway between Remedios and Aguacatán, a small country chapel with its windows boarded up, its pews and saints removed, but a simple cross remaining on a table near the head of the room opposite the entrance. That would have been the altar. Dozens of men and boys stood in the bare room—more than eighty, Pepe estimated aloud as they made their way toward the front of the room. A lot of the men seemed to know Pepe, although none of them were familiar to Nando. Six guerrillas stood in front of the table, wearing green uniforms, rifles strapped across their chests, and ski masks. They must have been hot, Nando thought. Years later he would remember the heat in the room. It was late in the dry season. He would remember ronrones buzzing in the wooden rafters. Their droning and the talking of the guerrillas made him sleepy. Land reform, village cooperative stores, clinics, free schools and textbooks for the poor—the talk was boring. Nando wanted to hear about battle plans.

Suddenly the lights went out. There were shouts, and movement all around them in the dark. Nando's boredom turned to confusion. Pepe grabbed his arm. "Let's go!"

They joined the rush toward the only door, Pepe carving a way through the crowd. Outside they were met by pandemonium—the roar of a helicopter and arriving jeeps, headlights blinding Nando. He made out soldiers leaping from the jeeps, running toward the mob from the meeting. He heard weapons firing, heard screaming, saw people falling. Pepe yanked him through the crowd that was breaking up in every direction. "This way!" Pepe ordered.

This would have been the moment for Nando to think, *Where's Memo?* But years later all he could remember was the sound of rotors and artillery and the terror that threatened to loosen his bowels. Pepe dragged him into the pinewoods behind the meeting house. It was pitch dark in the woods, except where the searchlight from the helicopter swept past, missing them. They ran, stumbling over brush and sticks, up the steep hill. They could hear others crashing through the woods around them. They couldn't tell if the sounds came from fellow escapees or from soldiers. They ran until Nando was gasping for breath. Pepe pulled him into a thicket. They flopped down and wormed on their bellies through tangled vines into the densest part of the brush, then lay still. "Memo?" Nando whispered.

"Ssh!" Pepe hissed.

This wasn't part of his plan. Or was it? Fernando wondered, years later.

They lay there as if paralyzed, listening to the crashing and shouts around them, more gunshots and screams, and the beating of the rotors. Rocks and sticks dug into Nando's stomach and his arms, which were folded to cradle his head, but he didn't dare shift to a more comfortable position. He felt like the snapping of a twig could give them away to the soldiers hunting through the woods. The helicopter circled and came in close over his head, its sound splitting his ears. The searchlight swept over them, lighting up the mosaic of leaves that hid them. Nando felt himself shrink from the light. He felt a hot flood of urine around his groin. He felt tears leak from his eyes and tried to blink them away. He could feel Pepe's body against him tremble. He tried to see his older brother lying beside him. Pepe's hand found his and squeezed it. The light moved on. Through the leaves he could see the men running in the woods. He saw bodies falling and heard shrieks. "Ayúdame Dios!" "Mami!"

The nightmare went on and on. The helicopter circled, the guns fired, the bodies fell. Nando smelled the stink of blood and shit and fear penetrate into his hiding place. The night was cold after the heat of the day. Nando's piss-soaked pants and shirt soon chilled him. His arms fell asleep, but still he didn't dare move them. He listened to the sounds in the forest. The helicopter circled. He heard thuds and curses. He heard screams, but no more shots. He didn't know what was happening outside his cocoon of safety. He let the tears stream down his face but was afraid to sniffle. The light from the helicopter flashed through the woods, then passed on. The drone of the helicopter faded. He listened to its beat receding. Now he could hear more clearly the cries and groans in the forest. He heard dragging noises. Sounds of artillery came from the direction of the safe house below them, then a boom and burst of flames. Smoke and the smell of gasoline and burning flesh made him gag. He craned his neck to peer through the branches at the glow from the fire.

The fire blazed. He heard the jeeps drive off. His body hurt everywhere; he longed to roll over, but still he didn't dare. He wished he could pass out and wake up at home, in his bed. The light from the fire died. His eyes adjusted to the darkness, and he could see the gleam of Pepe's eyes. Still they didn't speak. Nando's heart continued to pound. He felt a cramp in his side. He moved his body a little. In the silence, he listened for footsteps or voices but heard only the hoot of an owl. Pepe shifted beside him but didn't say anything, although Nando could see that he was awake. He waited for Pepe to give a signal. He thought about his mother. Would he ever see her again? He thought about Memo. Had he been killed? He heard rustlings in the undergrowth. He thought about ghosts. He heard a coyote howl. He thought about God and promised to go to confession. What other promises could he make? The night went on and on. Then it started to get light; Pepe rolled over and put his hand gently on Nando's back. "Time to go," he whispered.

They crawled out into the gray dawn, and Pepe helped him stand up and brush himself off. "Well, hermanito, did that scare the shit out of you?" Pepe said quietly. "I sure didn't expect it. We've been meeting for months with no problem. Someone must have talked."

"What do you think happened to Memo?"

"Let's hope he got away. But we can't look for him now. We need to get out of here. The soldiers will be back in the daylight to finish the job."

They didn't look around them for signs of the fight, but walked up into the hills through the dark forest, avoiding the roads. Pepe knew the way. It took them three hours to walk home. "What happened?" their mother cried when she saw them.

Nando couldn't talk. He went straight to bed. "Let him rest," Pepe said. Pepe left for Mexico that day. "Too many people know I've been going to meetings," he told the family. "Fernando should be OK, if he just stays in school." If his mother was angry at her firstborn, she was more relieved that both sons had survived. If she had fears for Nando, neither did she want to see all her sons flee, Fernando knew, looking back. The family had always lived in Remedios, always under one roof, surrounded by uncles and aunts and cousins. Doña Teresa couldn't imagine a world otherwise. And yet, by the time the Violence was over (Fernando would never stop calling the war by the name the people had given it, never switch over to the more clinical sounding *internal conflict* favored of late among sociologists and political commentators), her unimaginable had come to pass. Four of her children had left for Mexico and the United States; nine of her grandchildren were born there—lost to her, but survivors.

His father made Nando go back to school on Monday. When Anita asked if he knew where Memo was, his stomach churned and his chest tightened. "No. Don't you?" he managed to say.

Memo had disappeared.

1982

MEMO WAS IN THE SAFE HOUSE when the soldiers charged through the door. They came in firing. The dark chapel was still full of people from the meeting. Nando and his brother had disappeared. Memo heard thunderous blasts of gunfire and screams. He hit the floor and started inching away from the door and the soldiers, toward the side wall of the chapel.

Flashlights swept through the chaotic crowd. The soldiers surged in, no longer firing but using their weapons as clubs. Memo heard rifle butts slam against skulls, the cries and thuds of falling bodies. Outside a helicopter roared low over the building.

A light flashed in Memo's face. He looked up and saw a rifle pointed at him, but couldn't see beyond it to the soldier.

"Get up," a voice commanded.

Memo rose slowly and deliberately, his back against the chapel wall. The light moved up and down his body.

"What are you doing here?" the soldier asked. "You're dressed pretty fancy for a subversive."

Memo still had on his school uniform, although it was a Friday night. Most of the men at the meeting had come in tattered work clothes after a day in the fields. He thought hard about what answer could save his life. "I thought it was a recruitment meeting," he said. "I met a guy in the park this afternoon who told me the special forces were looking for recruits."

"What bullshit!" The soldier slapped him across the face, banging his head against the wall. "We recruit at the base. What the fuck would we be doing in this shithole in the middle of nowhere?"

His face stinging from the blow, Memo answered. "He said it was in a secret location because it wasn't a normal recruitment. He said it was for Kaibiles."

Memo had no idea how the special forces recruited.

A shout interrupted their exchange. "Attention! This is your lieutenant. All eyes up here! Look at this scum." Both Memo and his attacker turned to look.

Soldiers in camouflage surrounded the six guerrillas who moments before had been addressing the meeting, shining their lights on them. The lieutenant, a bull-necked man in a maroon beret, pulled the ski mask off a guerrilla. The other soldiers followed suit, baring haggard faces and hollow, unshaved cheeks. At the officer's command the soldiers dropped back, training their weapons on the guerrillas. Silence fell over the room, except for the moans of the wounded.

"Which one of you motherfucking Communists is the leader?" the lieutenant demanded.

The guerrillas hesitated and looked at each other. Memo saw them set their faces and shoulders in a show of bravery. One stepped forward. "That would be me."

"That would be you." The lieutenant spat loudly on the floor. "Very good, turd. What's that you've got slung around your shoulder?"

For the first time Memo realized that none of the guerrillas had fired their rifles, which were still strapped across their chests where he'd seen them at the beginning of the meeting. The guerrilla leader reached for his weapon.

"Freeze!" the lieutenant shouted, his face turning livid in the glow from the flashlights. The guerrilla froze. The lieutenant yanked at the weapon, breaking the flimsy strap. He gave a loud guffaw.

"As I thought. Painted wood. You're fighting a revolution with toy guns."

An intake of breaths hissed through the room. *Jesus, Mother Mary!* Memo thought.

"You're in church. It's time to pray, faggot. On your knees." The lieutenant struck the guerrilla on the back of his knees with the wooden rifle and he collapsed onto the floor. "Which one of you Indian dirtballs has a machete?" The officer peered around the dark room. Flashlights moved among the shadowy figures. Guarded by the soldier, Memo watched the flickering beams from the sidelines. It looked like more than half the people from the meeting were still there, trapped, and twice as many soldiers. A soldier pushed a campesino toward the lieutenant. He was a scrawny man in Indian clothes and a machete hung in a leather sheath from his belt.

"Have you ever butchered a sheep?" the lieutenant asked him.

"Señor?"

"I've been a farmer and I know, asshole. You've butchered a sheep."

"Yes." The peasant's voice was barely above a whisper, but could be heard in the silence of the room.

"Well then, a man is easier. Cut the head off this guerrilla."

Memo gasped.

"Señor!" The peasant shrank back. The soldier with him grabbed his arm and dragged him closer to the lieutenant and the kneeling guerrilla. All eyes were on the campesino. He fumbled with the sheath and withdrew his machete. It shook in his hands. "It's not sharp, my captain."

The officer's lips curled in a smile, perhaps at the inadvertent promotion. "Lend me your kerchief." He reached for the peasant's hat. The peasant flinched, expecting a blow, but the lieutenant lifted his hat, whipped off the bandana wrapped around his head, and replaced the hat with a nod. "Your service to your country will be remembered. You, Corporal!" he barked at the soldier guarding the campesino. "Blindfold the prisoner. Tie his hands."

He watched with the grin still on his face, like an actor enjoying center stage, while the corporal twisted the bandana around the eyes of the guerrilla kneeling at his feet. "Take a good look at your leader, faggots," he said, flashing his light on the other guerrillas. "Your turn will be next."

The soldier finished tying the prisoner's hands behind his back and stepped away.

"Now! Try to do it in one clean slice." The smile faded from the lieutenant's face and he trained his beam on the peasant once more. The campesino hesitated and looked around the room, seeking any escape. The corporal raised his rifle and trained it on the peasant. "Now," the lieutenant repeated. "I'm getting impatient."

The campesino grasped the machete with both hands and raised it over his head. The guerrilla knelt with his forehead against the floor, as if bowing to a pitiless god. Memo looked for a tremble in the bound hands against his back, or a shudder in his exposed neck, to betray his terror. Where could his thoughts be? The campesino swung the machete down on the back of the prisoner's neck with a dull thwack. A strangled "Ahhhh…" followed by gurgling sounds issued from the guerrilla. Blood gushed from the neck, but the head was still attached. "Motherfucker!" the lieutenant shouted. "You botched it, pubic hair!"

He grabbed the machete from the peasant's hand and pushed him away, then hacked at the severed neck, grunting as he did so. The guerrilla's spasming body fell sideways; the lieutenant continued hacking, until the head finally fell away in a pool of blood. A bright flashlight illuminated the guerrilla's open mouth twitching in the bloody tangle of beard, still seeming to attempt a scream. Memo clenched his teeth so he would not vomit.

"That's the way it's done, asshole." The lieutenant shoved the bloodied machete back at the peasant, then leaned over to pick up the guerrilla's head by its coarse black hair. He raised it, peeled off the blindfold, and displayed the head to the other guerrillas, standing nearby riveted with horror. The lieutenant's back was turned toward Memo, and he could no longer see the face of the dead guerilla, just the dripping, tattered flesh at the base of the head.

"Which one of you cowards is ready to follow your leader?" The lieutenant tossed the head toward one of the guerrillas, who in a startled reflex caught it as if it were a soccer ball. "Bravo!" The lieutenant clapped, then took two steps toward the guerrilla and grabbed the head from his hands. He smashed the head against the floor, stomping it with his boot. Memo winced. "Your turn will come, shitface. But first you're going to headquarters for questioning. Take them out," the lieutenant ordered, indicating the remaining guerrillas. "Dispose of the subversives. Don't waste ammunition." The lieutenant followed the guerrillas down the length of the church toward the door. The soldiers and their victims moved out of his way.

Years later, after his training had inured him to the sight of blood and brutality, Memo would be able to recall with perfect clarity his sensations in that moment, the pounding of his heart, his gasping for breath, even as his mind fought to block out sensation. He knew that his life depended on it. He steeled himself and looked at his captor, who was watching him with narrowed eyes. He had dark skin and Indian features. "You still want to be a Kaibil, fancypants?"

"Yes," Memo said. "Tell me what I have to do."

"Call me Sergeant, punk." He pointed to the stripes on his beret.

"Sergeant, sir." Memo didn't allow a tremor in his voice.

"You have to throw away the books. Must be nice, sitting in a comfortable classroom, keeping your hands clean." The sergeant's Spanish was clumsy and butchered, uneducated. "You're going to miss that, aren't you?" He waited for an answer. The answer seemed important. One wrong inflection and the soldier would stop asking questions and join in the frenzied beating that had resumed when the lieutenant left.

"I can't afford the fees. I'm dropping out. That's why I want to enlist." He wanted to dispel the impression that he was a rich kid. He sensed the man's resentment.

"Any shitball can enlist. To be a Kaibil, you have to survive sixty days in the University of Hell. You have to swim through mud and excrement, drink the sludge of burnt artillery shells, dig bullets out of your own flesh." The brute looked pleased with his list. "Book learning won't help you. You see this Galil?" He aimed his automatic rifle at Memo, sighted it, and stared. Memo's pulse jumped. Then he noted that the sergeant hadn't cocked the rifle. His pulse steadied. The soldier lowered the weapon. "This is your professor." He looked around, suddenly in a hurry. "Come with me."

Still not knowing what the sergeant's intentions were, Memo stuck close to his side. They made their way toward the door past writhing bodies, flailing clubs, shouted curses and supplications. He heard men sobbing and begging for their lives and calling out to God and the Virgin Mary as they were struck down. He looked for Nando and his brother, but they were nowhere to be seen.

Outside the temperature had dropped. The cold night air felt refreshing after the heat inside. Above the headlights of the idling jeeps and trucks that surrounded the chapel, he saw stars.

He and the sergeant climbed into the back of an army truck where five other youths from the meeting stood guarded by Galil-toting soldiers. The sergeant lashed his wrists and tied them to the metal bars that enclosed the back of the truck in a cage. "The show is almost over," he said. "I don't want you to miss the fireworks." He'd tied him facing the chapel, as were all the men in the truck.

His captor lit a cigarette. They watched soldiers pour out of the building and race up into the woods behind the chapel. They saw lights flashing through the trees and heard machine guns firing and grenades exploding. They watched the helicopter circle and saw soldiers coming back down out of the forest dragging bodies—alive or dead, Memo couldn't tell—toward the door of the chapel. The sergeant finished his cigarette, threw it down, and jumped out of the truck, yelling a command. Two of the other soldiers followed, leaving two to guard the bound captives. Memo didn't dare speak. The two guards talked to each other in a Mayan language from a different region. Memo wondered if any of his fellow captives could understand them and knew any more about what was in store for them than he did. The other captives appeared young and fit like him. They also maintained a stony silence. He hoped they had all been selected for conscription, not for torture and death.

Memo's hands were numb from the tight ropes, his head ached from the cold, and his legs felt like they might buckle at any moment, when the sergeant reappeared over the back of the truck. Soldiers were running toward the vehicles from the chapel. His captor clapped Memo on the back. "The subversives are all inside," he said. "Keep your eye on the church door."

The door was standing open, a black rectangle in the white wall illuminated by headlights. There was no longer any movement inside the church, no more screams emanating from it. Were they all dead? With a sudden boom the church's interior ignited in a fireball. The last of the soldiers ran toward the jeeps, carrying gasoline cans. The air filled with smoke and the smell of burning flesh. Memo was torn between relief that he wasn't inside the inferno and dread. Engines revved all around them. He didn't dare ask where they were going.

As if in answer to his unvoiced question, the sergeant spoke. "It's back to the base. You've just learned your first lesson. Scorched earth."

5

2012

FERNANDO AND MEMO sat on the veranda of the Pink House looking out over the tangled garden, with its jungle of bougainvillea and rampant roses, and below it the flat fields of the valley ending in hills and rolling mountains. Thunderheads hung over a distant volcano. Fernando poured Scotch into a glass and handed it to Memo. "Salud!" he said. "To your health."

"And yours," Memo said. His lips twitched.

"I don't usually get out here without the whole family. It's a treat." Sandra had looked at him with raised eyebrows when he took the SUV after lunch and told her where he was going.

"Alone?" she'd asked. If the kids didn't go with him, usually his brothers did.

"Memo and I have some catching up to do," he'd said. He tried to sound offhand about it. He didn't want her to know, didn't even want to admit to himself, that he was scared. He didn't know who scared him more: the Rattlesnake or Memo.

"Are you finding life here a change of pace?" he asked Memo. "I suppose it's an ideal spot for contemplation." He imagined Memo's normal pace was anything but contemplative.

"Ideal," Memo agreed. He leaned back in his chair looking comfortable. His jeans were pressed, Fernando noticed, and looked expensive. Fernando's slacks were cheap polyester, a nondescript dark color suitable for country or town since he would be teaching later that day.

"Not too lonely?" Fernando asked, hoping to disguise his anxiety as concern for his guest. "No one gets out here except on weekends." Last weekend they had deliberately stayed in town, out of respect for Memo's stated desire for solitude, not wanting to subject him right away to the boisterous crowd of children and garrulous uncles. Only Sandra had been out a few times, to check on their guest and bring him supplies. "Not too boring?"

"It suits me. I get the feeling you'd find it dull. You're looking for a little excitement perhaps?" Memo's deep-set eyes pierced him, reading his hidden thoughts.

"Maybe not excitement," Fernando said. "But a new venture of some kind. Some…investments I made went…bad. That and the new addition on the house. You know a college professor doesn't make a fortune." He gave a dry laugh. His sister and brother-in-law did better out of their tiny grocery in a room of their house a block from his than he did with all his advanced degrees. "The truth is, I'm in a jam."

"Ah. I remember you as a risk-taker." Memo smiled.

Fernando felt a chill, wondering what memories he referred to. "Only once or twice, and it didn't turn out well." It was way too late to apologize, and he didn't know if an apology was wanted. "You'd think I would learn."

The sound of grinding gears carried in the quiet. Off to their right, across the river, a truck crawled up the highway that climbed the face of the Cuchumatanes, struggling at the point where the road made the first of a number of hairpin turns. "Do they still call that switchback the Zeta?" Memo asked. He said the name of the letter easily enough, as if it didn't now have an altogether different significance.

"Yes, and the road still washes out in every rainy season."

Clouds were lowering onto the high plateau, and the day was darkening. "Looks like it might rain." Memo said.

"The farmers would like that." He and his brothers hired a local peasant to plant their fields. The young corn was stunted by the drought.

"How much of this land belongs to your family?" Memo asked.

"My brothers' plots go down to that line of trees." Fernando indicated a spot halfway down the valley. "The white house beyond them belongs to my cousin."

"The one you don't get along with."

Fernando looked surprised. Memo added, "Your wife told me, when she brought me out here. A dispute over water, she said."

"My cousin is an asshole. He's trying to grow greenhouse tomatoes in the dry season."

"It's good flat land," Memo said. "A small chemical factory would do well here. One that doesn't require water, and is safe and non-polluting."

Fernando studied Memo, who gazed off at the distant volcano with an unreadable expression.

"What kind of chemical do you have in mind?"

"A pharmaceutical. Very profitable if one is discreet." Memo helped himself to more Johnny Walker and poured some into Fernando's glass. Thunder rumbled.

"Is there risk?" Fernando felt his heart palpitating. He took a large swallow of whisky to quiet down his internal organs.

"We would call it cleaning supplies. The tricky thing is getting some of the necessary ingredients past government restrictions. Theoretically you need a permit to import them.

Methylamine and phenyl acetic acid." He reeled off names that meant nothing to Fernando but sounded menacing. It was as if Memo was testing his knowledge of chemistry. Fernando was afraid to ask, afraid to reveal his ignorance. More than that, he was afraid to know. "They come from China," Memo said. "Fortunately, I have a port connection down on the coast."

Nothing good came out of China. The warning signs were everywhere. Fernando felt himself rushing toward disaster. "We're far from the coast," he observed.

"That's an advantage. It's less obvious. Plus, we're close to Mexico. For export." Memo leaned back in his chair and sipped his Scotch. "It's just an idea. If you're not interested, we can forget it."

That wasn't true. This project would take place somehow, somewhere nearby, with or without him, Fernando was sure. He wouldn't be able to forget that he was being offered a position, a chance to get out of his hole, a shot at independence. If he passed it up, would he look back with regret? Memo would find someone else. Fernando would have squandered the opportunity being dropped into his lap. "I'm interested. But…I don't have a lot of capital to put into it."

"No. You provide this house, and the land where we construct a modest warehouse. I'll lease the house and land from you and your brothers. I have a little nest egg I've saved, and various sponsors who will invest with me. In addition to the rent, you'll get a share of the profits." The project seemed well thought out.

"Hmm. I'll have to speak to my brothers."

"Take your time. I'm sure you can be persuasive." Memo smiled again. "We have another advantage here. An old friend of mine is commander of the base in Huehue. We were together in the Petén. I paid him a call this week. We should have no problems with security."

Fernando turned this over in his thoughts. So Memo had left the army on good terms, it seemed. Perhaps some of the rumors he'd heard were untrue. Or perhaps not.

"When you were training for the Kaibiles?" he asked, then kicked himself. The Scotch had loosened his tongue. The last thing he wanted at this point in the discussion was to bring up Memo's military career, and his own part in it. Memories of the night of the guerrilla meeting had come flooding back since Memo's return. He didn't know what had happened to Memo that night, and he was afraid to ask. He didn't know if Memo blamed him. On the other hand, he'd come back to Huehue and sought out Fernando. That had to be a good sign.

A bolt of lightning leapt out of the clouds at the foot of the valley, followed by a crack of thunder. The air turned cold. The sky opened in a downpour.

"The farmers will be pleased," Memo said over the drumming of rain on the tile roof.

They went inside, where it was drier. By the time the rain had stopped, the Johnny Walker bottle was empty. Despite that, the subject of the Kaibiles hadn't come up again. Fernando left, with no more clues to how Memo had spent the last thirty years than he'd had before, from that brief glimpse when Memo had brought down the dove with the slingshot. He concentrated on steering the SUV over the rough road that the downpour had turned from dust to mud. The channels in the riverbed that he'd crossed without thinking on the way in were now raging torrents. He picked his way and forced the vehicle through the current. Brown water swirled up to the bumper, but the engine didn't stall. Climbing out of the river his tires churned and slid in the mud. He was glad to reach the paved road and breathed a sigh of relief. He'd escaped from one devil. On to the next.

Halfway between Remedios and Huehue, he pulled into a gas station, parked, and went inside the low cinderblock building. "Is he here?" he asked the woman behind the wooden counter with its display of unappetizing pastries.

"Soon," she said. She was a stumpy, dark woman with bristles on her cheeks. Strange, thought Fernando, that the Rattlesnake would have such an ugly wife. No doubt he saved himself for his girlfriends.

"I'll have a coffee," he told her. He needed to sober up before his evening class.

She poured a cup of the watery brew, stirred in the sugar, and handed it to him just as the Rattlesnake rolled in. The name didn't fit the man, not with his big belly protruding from his open leather jacket and his soft puffy jowls. There were some who claimed his rattle was worse than his bite, but Fernando didn't want to find out. The gold chain that gleamed through his chest hair flaunted his impunity. He didn't have to worry about thieves, or personal safety. "Fernando," he said, and nodded toward the inner door. Fernando followed him into the back room and stood while the Rattlesnake removed his expensive cowboy hat and settled into a spindly chair behind the desk. "My friend. Good to see you after too long. I've been waiting."

He didn't sound friendly. He sounded impatient.

Fernando took a roll of bills out of his pocket and smoothed them onto the desk. "My payment," he said. In fact it was Memo's first payment, on the rental of the house and land. The Rattlesnake's fat fingers flicked greedily through the bills.

"Almost two weeks late," he said when he'd finished count-ing twice, blowing heavily through his walrus moustache. "I thought I was going to have to send you a reminder. Have I mentioned to you what my reminders are?"

"I won't be late again," Fernando said. This monthly ritual, which had begun midway through the renovation when Fer-nando's savings gave out and the builder's expenses kept rising, was wearing him down. The Rattlesnake enjoyed giving recita-tions of escalating violence, beginning with broken kneecaps and crushed fingers.

"The first of the month, Don Fernando. That's when I'm paid. I run a business."

"You'll be paid. With your permission, I have to go. My students are waiting."

"Let them wait. Don't make me wait. Adios, amigo." Chuck-ling at his own wit, the loan shark waved Fernando out of the office. He was out of the Rattlesnake's clutches. And into Memo's.

After Fernando taught his class he sat at his computer in his office with the door closed to research chemicals. What he learned about the dangers of methamphetamine production gave him no comfort. The *Prensa Libre* indicated that it was still a small-scale venture in Guatemala, limited to mobile labs carried around in the backs of trucks. But authorities in Mexico were finding industrial super-labs in large warehouses turn-ing out huge quantities of crystal meth. Tons of the drug were flowing north—Fernando tried to picture how much space a ton of crystals would take up—to fill the supply gap left when the US had managed to cut down on its domestic production.

He pictured large nondescript warehouses stocked with cleaning supplies, like the one Memo was planning to build on his property.

The articles in *Prensa Libre* included gruesome descriptions of what the drug did to its users—rotting their teeth, sending them into fits of screaming paranoia, stopping their hearts. He shuddered. Well, the saving grace about the addicts: they were far away. Of immediate concern was the pressure and money coming from the US to bolster drug law enforcement in Guatemala.

But Memo had reassured him on that score. He had more to fear from Memo's Mexican "sponsors" than the Guatemalan army. His head ached. Too much Scotch in the afternoon. He shut down the computer and slipped it into his briefcase, locked his office, and headed out into the night. The stars were out and the air fresh and clean after the rain.

Over a quiet supper—it was late, and the kids were already in their rooms—he told his brothers that a small ecological cleaning supply factory was just what they needed out at Sapoclok. "Simple economics! Since free trade with the United States, there's no money in planting corn. Imported is cheaper than locally grown." It was only fair to trade back with a product the North Americans wanted, he thought. This thought shamed him. It was no secret to himself that he was desperate. "We only plant corn because we've always done it."

When they asked him for details on the cleaning supply plant he said, "You'll have to talk to Memo. He's the brains of the operation. I teach social theory."

"We don't know much about Memo," Elías pointed out.

"What's to know? He's not asking us for money. The reverse."

"What about Pepe?" Their oldest brother in Mexico owned the Pink House and the fields immediately surrounding it, including the avocado orchard. He'd always let the family use it freely.

Fernando felt a pang. He'd never lost his veneration for his big brother, and regretted that he didn't get along with Pepe's wife. None of the brothers did. Fernando hated family discord. "We'll still plant corn on his land," he said. "And harvest avocados." Another product that cost more to harvest than its yield paid. "I'll talk to him. He already gave me permission to rent the house to Memo." Without hesitation Pepe had said, "Of course, Nando. You know I trust your judgment." Fernando would hate to betray that trust.

Luis, just back from San Cristóbal, where Pepe and their sister Emilia lived in Mexico, said, "He wants to sell the house. He's never coming back. His children are Mexican. They don't want to leave Mexico. And he doesn't want to leave them."

"In that case, we can buy him out with the profits from the plant," Fernando said.

"If there are any profits," Elías said. Elías was a businessman, the only one at the table. "There's a big gap between dreams and reality, let me warn you."

Sandra got up to clear plates, the maid having gone home for the day. "I have to put Leti and Walter to bed." She left business discussions to the men. She would listen. Later, when they were alone, she would give Fernando her opinion, and it was sure to be reasoned and forceful.

After she left the men remained at the table, drinking coffee. Edgar said, "You know, I'd been thinking of building my own little house on my plot." Since retiring from teaching elementary school, Edgar had been at loose ends, needing a project to fill his time.

"You still can," Fernando said. "Build on the pine ridge, with a view of the valley."

"A view of a factory?" Edgar's tone revealed skepticism.

"An attractive building surrounded by lemon trees. Think of it as an industrial park, very modern. No noise, no pollution. Come out to the Pink House with me on Sunday and Memo will explain the whole thing." To his relief, they agreed to take that first step, reserving final judgment on the project until after they'd met with Memo.

That night he lay in bed and felt Sandra's warmth beside him. It was dark in the room with the shutters closed. Tired as he was, he couldn't sleep. The confidence he'd projected earlier in the evening melted away in the dark. He moved closer to Sandra and spooned her slender body, feeling it through her silky nightgown. He put his palm against her ribcage, under her breasts, and snuggled her against his soft belly. She breathed evenly. He smelled her faintly sour hair, so familiar, so comforting. In eighteen years of marriage he'd never betrayed her. He was not a mujeriego like his father and so many of his friends. He'd felt early on the painful effects of his father's philandering; it didn't appeal to him, even though university life offered plenty of opportunities, pretty young girls willing to trade a tryst with their professor for a better grade. He avoided temptation and held fast to a known quantity. If his sex life was a little boring, having the companionship of his competent, reliable wife made up for it. He valued her trust. Particularly when he was feeling doubts. "Are you awake, love?" he asked, knowing that she wasn't. She'd already been asleep when he came upstairs after the long discussion with his brothers.

She stirred and wove her fingers through his hand on her chest. "Mmmm?"

"You've been out to the Pink House a few times since Memo got here. What's your impression?"

"Impression, my love?" She was awake now.

"Of Memo. Does he talk about me?"

"He's not very talkative. Why?"

"I just wondered," Fernando said. "You know, he came straight to me, first thing he got back to Huehue. I wonder why."

"Weren't you very close, back when you were boys?"

"Well yes...and no. Not so much toward the end." He'd never told Sandra the story. "Does he talk about the past?"

"No. He asks questions."

"What about?" There it was again, the feeling of uneasiness. At least with the Rattlesnake, you knew who you were dealing with, a small-time crook with only local connections.

"The neighbors, the family, people around town. What are you worried about, Fernando?" There was worry in her voice now too. She'd been against the addition to the house when he first proposed it, wanting to save the money for the children's educations. Then when he got the loan, she'd been reassured and had joined into planning the airy rooms and lavish bathrooms and wide stairways and big windows with enthusiasm. She thought the loan had come from the bank. She didn't know the banks had stopped lending. She didn't know about the Rattlesnake.

"Nothing," he said, squeezing her fingers. "Go back to sleep." He pressed his nose into her hair and gave a deep sigh.

6

EARLY ON A WEEKDAY MORNING the citizens of Remedios appeared to have all the time in the world to stop for a shoeshine under one of the umbrellas that lined the edge of the central park, or to chat with a fruit vendor or a woman sweeping up dead leaves and fallen bougainvillea blossoms from the park pathways, or to dawdle by the fountain before heading into the municipal building. This square was the heart and soul of Remedios—an old soul, little changed since colonial times, its façades colonial gold and terra cotta. It was Remedios's central nervous system as well; every seemingly lazy interaction was in fact the communication of information among the denizens of the town, information that would be disseminated through the veins and arteries of the organism, reaching its farthest flung extremities before the day's end. The door of the colonial church opened onto the square in an invitation to step inside. Some mornings Sandra would stop in for a little prayer, an oasis of spirituality in her busy day, some private time with God, but not today. Today, having just relinquished her two middle children to the nun at the school entrance, she passed the church at a clip. The force that impelled her was not something she wanted to expose to the eyes of God or priest, far less to the whispers of her neighbors. All the world thought of her as a good wife, a good mother, a good Catholic. No one really knew her. Not Fernando who, after waking her up last night to ask her about Memo and subject her to a terrifying instant of shame and remorse, had dropped off to sleep, loudly snoring, enveloping her in his cushiony embrace. Not Fernando's brothers, who blundered in and out of rooms all day without knocking. Not his sisters, aunts, and female cousins whose houses pressed in on hers from every side, not even with their womanly clairvoyance.

The clock in the colonial tower of the municipal building began tolling, its chimes audible all over town. When they were first courting Fernando had taken her to see its pendulum, accessed by an ancient winding wooden staircase open to the public. Eight chimes rang out with the slow inevitability of the day that stretched before her, mechanical in its predictability.

Predictability that had come out of nowhere. The first time she took Memo out to the Pink House, two weeks ago but it felt much longer, an attack of physical attraction had taken her by surprise. It came from some animal deep inside her she hadn't known existed. A fer-de-lance coiled behind her sex, startled awake by Memo's cap of tight curls, his hooded eyes, his warrior's physique, even—she had to admit it—by the awe her husband held for Memo's myth. She'd been making his bed and he offered to help. His hands smoothed the sheets as if they were her skin. She wanted to feel those hands on her body.

She'd always had an aversion to being handled. Early boyfriends kissed her, but she made sure they kept their hands in safe zones. She'd hoped Fernando would transport her to ecstasy, as promised in the magazines and telenovelas. Instead, his probing in her intimate places felt like an invasion. She decided that sex was overrated. She went through the motions and waited for it to be over.

She had stared at Memo's hands on the sheets, barely able to breathe. She'd never even heard of him until he'd showed up at her house for lunch. He'd never figured in Fernando's stories of his childhood. The stories spilled out the night after Memo arrived—the poor boy who had dazzled Fernando with his soccer skills and become a high school legend, then disappeared in the Violencia, Fernando didn't know how or where. Sandra sensed a mystery. There were rumors that Memo was dangerous, but Fernando downplayed these. She felt the danger, uncoiling in her depths. Across the bed from Memo, she met his eyes and felt herself blush. Did Memo sense her lust? She vowed to contain her fear and see what happened.

Two days later, she went back to the Pink House. To drop off a pot of chiles rellenos for Memo to put in his fridge, that was her excuse. She took Omar with her this time, her two-year-old guard against the fer-de-lance. Omar sat on Memo's lap while she made them coffee. Memo played patty cake with him, holding Omar's little hands in his big ones and slapping them together chanting, "Tortillitas for Mamá, tortillitas for Papá." Omar squealed with glee. "The pretty ones for Mamá, the burnt ones for Papá." Again Sandra found herself mesmerized by Memo's hands, hands that she imagined had killed people, his long, delicate fingers cupped around Omar's chubby wrists.

"You're good with him," she said, putting his coffee on the table where Omar couldn't reach it. "You should have some of your own."

"What makes you think that I don't?" Memo said, tickling Omar to keep him laughing. Memo's face was serious.

"Oh…" Sandra paused, aware that she was prying into his personal history. "Something you said to Fernando. I just assumed. I guess it's none of my business."

"I had a wife and three kids in Mexico. I lost them. An accident."

"Oh!" Sandra sank into her chair, appalled, feeling ashamed of her curiosity. "I can't imagine losing my children. It must be the most terrible thing. I'm sorry." What kind of accident could destroy a whole family? A car accident? Or something more sinister, less accidental. She couldn't ask him, she didn't dare. Rather, she felt him looking into her, her attraction to him deepened by tragedy.

"Thank you," he said, then smiled at Omar. His smile lifted her mood. "This one looks just like his mother. Very beautiful."

She went hot at the compliment. Before she could think of a reply, Memo lifted Omar off his lap, stood him up and grabbed his fists. He jabbed them forward and back in play boxing moves. "We must toughen you up, little guy. Beauty is good for women; not for men."

She laughed, a little too loud, a little too delighted, and then resumed her normal demeanor with an effort, and put on her hostess face. "You flatter me. But I know it's my chiles rellenos you're really after."

"Of course," he said.

Nothing more had happened that day. She knew it was only a matter of time, if she kept going back. Caution kept her away. She tallied up what she had to lose if she gave in to temptation. Everything. She would be banned from the sacrament, driven from her home. Her children would be expelled from Catholic school and barred from seeing her, forced to accept a stepmother when Fernando found a new wife. Still she felt the deadly snake writhing in her, trying to break free.

She had finally gone back, two days ago. They'd gone out behind the house. Memo had held the gate for her, saying, "Come for a walk?"

The spicy aroma of pine needles had risen around them as she followed him uphill into the woods, panting a little. They had reached the ridge in the heat of afternoon. He had stopped, looked back down at her, and smiled in the mysterious way he had. "Have you been to the place the locals call the Green Lagoon?" he'd asked.

She had. It was a place of family picnics. "You've gone far," she had said.

"I've had time." He'd set off on the path that descended into the ravine, entering groves of pine and alder. It was so private in the shady woods, in the deep ravine, far from habitations, no shepherds or flocks, anything could have happened. She'd followed him, slipping on dry leaves as they climbed up the opposite bank. He'd caught her hand and helped her up, holding her hand, his touch lingering, protecting her, as they walked in silence. "Careful," he'd said when he loosened his grip at the brow of the next hill.

He'd led her on through the pines, through twists and turnoffs in the path, skirting more ravines, crossing a small meadow, until they came to a crest, where they had looked down at the small sluggish pond tucked into a pocket of the woods, emerald and singing with insects. Murk floated on its surface. "Tired?" Memo had asked, lowering himself to a hummock soft with pine needles and patting the ground beside him. She'd sat down, not too close, resisting as long as possible.

"Does all this belong to your husband's family?" he'd asked. And why had he reminded her of her husband just then? The last thing she wanted to think of in this fertile, redolent setting was Fernando, the landowner, and his cousins squabbling over boundaries.

"Down to that fence by the stream," she'd said. Below reeds at the bottom of the lagoon, wet lush grass covered the banks of a shallow stream. Sandra remembered the thick heavy silence that had wrapped them in its moist embrace.

Nothing had happened.

This morning, she'd told Fernando her parents had an old TV she wanted to take out to the Pink House. "Good idea," he'd said, flipping her the keys to the SUV. Before leaving for work in her car he gave her an easy kiss, the kiss of a man who has complete confidence in his good wife. Nothing of the inner battle she was waging had broken through her surface, she was sure. "I have meetings this afternoon, won't be home until late. Be careful crossing the river, my love."

The clock finished its chiming and she hurried home on foot. Several blocks from the church she passed through the cobbled square where these days buses parked but where the horse and oxen market had been held in Fernando's childhood. Sandra was from Huehue, the city so close but worlds away, and had heard every detail of Remedios's history and Fernando's childhood (or so she thought) so intimately entwined. The hot sun was beating down on the treeless square; the sky was washed clean by yesterday's rain. The rainy season had begun. Cloudless now, more than likely there would be another downpour this afternoon, possibly marooning her at the Pink House. Up the street she reached home and let herself in. Omar rocketed toward her from the kitchen, where Antonia was washing up the breakfast dishes. "Mami! Mami!"

"Let's go. We don't want Félix to be late." The day urged her on toward its predestined outcome. Félix tossed his school backpack into the back of the SUV. She strapped Omar into his car seat and circled around to the passenger door. "You drive, Félix. You need the practice."

Her oldest son, tall, broad-shouldered and full-bodied—now looking so much like Fernando when she'd first met him, her handsome young professor—folded himself into the driver's seat. He backed the SUV out of the driveway, through the gate, turning into the narrow street.

"Don't go too fast," she warned him. It always made her nervous to let him drive. She still felt like he was her precious baby boy. The first year of his life she'd been overwhelmed by love. Her passion for her newborn had eclipsed all previous loves and focused her senses on Félix, his gleaming chestnut waves, his pale cheeks, burrowing into her breasts. She'd nursed each subsequent baby with fierce devotion but none had matched the intoxication of the first. It had frightened her at the time; her love for her baby had felt adulterous in comparison with her love for Fernando. Maybe that was what was the matter with her. The vacuum left in her heart by Félix, growing up. Soon she'd be losing him to his simpering girlfriend.

"Don't worry, Mamá. I'm always extra careful when we have the baby." To prove it, he slowed the car almost to a stop to climb the first of the oversized speed bumps between Remedios and Huehue. His tone to her was invariably tender and protective, a model son. He took his special short cut to avoid the traffic jams, waited patiently at the lights, finally pulling up to the entrance of Francisco Javier, the same high school his father had attended. "See you later, Mamita," he said, getting out of the SUV.

"What time shall I pick you up?" Sandra asked, moving into the driver's seat.

He bent down to kiss her on both cheeks through the car window. "I'm going over to Gloria's after school, to help her with math."

Sandra sighed. "Don't stay late," she said. He was seventeen. She couldn't object, she had no grounds, and she couldn't bring herself to tell him how much she disliked his girlfriend. Fernando claimed she was jealous. She drove away fighting her feeling of loss. Memo's face flashed in her imagination. The desire in her loins stirred. Omar babbled in the back seat and she pushed the image away.

Her parents lived in a walled community on a hill on the outskirts of Huehue, just up from the evangelical church where her father was part of the lay ministry. She stopped in on them once or twice a week when the children were in school, both because it was expected and out of tenderness for her beleaguered mother. Her father would be home. A captain on the police force, he was working his preferred shift this week—afternoon and evening. Mornings bored him—not enough crime.

The atmosphere of her parents' house couldn't have been more different from that of the exuberant Granados household. She held Omar's hand and steered him past her mother's formal flower garden where there were no abandoned plastic trucks or muddy dolls sprawled among the perfect roses, or gaping holes dug by the dog. She confined him safely in the high chair while her mother served coffee in dainty cups on white lace doilies. She gave him a spoon to play with; even a piece of bread or cookie would end up spoiling the pristine whiteness of the tile floors. Her father looked pained when Omar banged the spoon on his plastic tray.

"Does he have to do that?"

"Papá!" Sandra snapped, her patience frazzled by her eagerness to be on her way. "You should be grateful you have grandsons."

"Of course I am. But you girls weren't so noisy."

"They were girls, Alejandro," her mother interceded. "Girls are naturally docile."

Sandra didn't remember it being so natural. She remembered her father's iron rule—not easy-going like Fernando, patient like Edgar, rambunctious like Luis. She remembered Biblical lectures, the sting and humiliation of his strap, being sent to bed without supper. But she didn't want to argue with her parents today. She wanted to be the good daughter for once.

"That guy who's staying out at Fernando's country place, what's he doing there? The word down at headquarters is that he's a drug dealer." Her father knew how to raise her alarm, almost as if he had looked into her soul.

"People are saying that about everyone now." She tried to stay calm and pick her words. "Is there any evidence?" Should she tell him that Memo wanted to build a chemical plant on their land? She'd heard the brothers discussing it before she went up to bed. She didn't know what it meant. Fernando had presented it as a straightforward business proposition. Drug traffickers didn't build factories; they smuggled marijuana and cocaine in armed convoys. They lived in mansions surrounded by bodyguards, not alone in small country houses. But something had made Fernando wake her up in the night with uncomfortable questions about Memo. After her initial panic had subsided and she'd realized that her traitorous attraction was not the issue, she'd lain awake wondering what was on his mind. She knew Fernando so well. Was it possible that he also had secrets? "Fernando trusts Memo," she said.

Did he? "He was in the special forces. Doesn't that put him above suspicion?"

Her father snorted. "Quite a few Kaibiles have gone over. The cartels pay better. This country is stinking with corruption, from generals and presidents down to the guys in my precinct whose palms are greased. Like that Jorge Mendoza, boasting about his kid in medical school. Now there's a man who's found creative ways to augment a policeman's salary!"

If he was so incorruptible, how had her father managed to send three daughters to college and build this house in the colonia?

"You don't know who you can trust any more," her mother said. As if you ever could, Sandra thought.

"*I* know who to trust." Her father's face flushed and his eyes took on a telltale glow. Sandra didn't want him to launch into an evangelizing tirade. They had reached a hard-won peace on the subject of religion since the day, when she was fourteen, that the Catholic priest had come knocking on their door. It must have been a Saturday because she wasn't in school or in church. Church, since they had left Catholicism to become Evangelicals, lasted all day. From her parent's bedroom where she was watching TV Sandra had heard the dog barking and her father's angry voice. She had come out of the bedroom and seen her father blocking the open doorway. She'd seen Father Giacomo outside, staring in at her.

"Get out!" her father had shouted. "Blasphemer! Idol worshipper! Papal toady! Out before I sic the dog on you!"

"Don Alejandro, please listen." Father Giacomo had looked from her father to Sandra, giving away her presence behind her father. "I was worried about your daughter. She missed the last confirmation class. I thought she might be sick. But I see she's looking fine."

Her father had turned around to glare at Sandra. She could still remember how he had enlarged in her vision with apocalyptic rage. "Confirmation class? *You*, Sandra? What is this?"

She had quaked, not knowing what to say. "All the girls were going, Papi. I…didn't want to be different."

She *did* want to be different from her father. This was her tenuous rebellion, fomented in secret, her revolution against the tyranny of those long Sundays dominated by him. Her mother had defended her. Coming out from the kitchen at the ruckus she had put a calming hand on her husband's arm and said in a firm voice, "Father, please come in. Won't you have some fresh shekas? I've just come from the bakery."

What had followed was a tense half hour in the dining room while Doña Lidia and Father Giacomo attempted to converse on noncontroversial topics. Don Alejandro and Sandra had sat in silence, the one angry, the other terrified. Later, her mother somehow convinced Don Alejandro to permit his middle daughter to leave the fold and rejoin the Catholic Church, replacing fire and brimstone with candles, incense, and soul-satisfying ritual.

"Papá, won't you come to Grandparents' Day at school next week?" she said. "It would mean so much to Walter and Leti."

"Of course we'll come," Doña Lidia said. Despite her aversion to Catholic school, her mother wouldn't neglect her grandchildren. Don Alejandro grunted his disapproval.

"It's time I run," Sandra said, relieved that the visit had lasted long enough that she could leave. Her father carried the TV set out to the SUV. She drove back to Remedios and dropped Omar off at home. It was time for his nap. Tona would take care of him and the children's lunch. There was nothing more tying her to duty, nothing preventing her from going in the direction she was headed. She changed into a prettier blouse and slapped on mascara and lipstick, quickly, furtively, hiding from herself and Tona what she was doing. She pulled out of her driveway and Tona shut the gate behind her. She said to herself: *This is it.*

She half expected people on the street to turn and stare at her, as if she were already guilty of transgression and everybody knew it. As if everyone she passed knew whose car this was and where it was bound and for what. She rolled up the car's windows to hide behind the tinted glass. She passed the water tank with its public washing sinks long dry and out of use, Don Lico's corner store, the gas station and truckers' hotel owned by Solomeros purportedly laundering drug money; every spot along the route was familiar and dear, as if she were seeing it for the last time as a virtuous woman. Outside of Doña Severina's little luncheonette the tall poinsettias had finally dropped their red petals, a reminder that Easter and redemption were long past. Her hands on the steering wheel and her foot on the gas were resolute when she turned off the paved road and barreled over ruts, past front doors left open to let the children in and out. "Doña Sandra, how are you, where are you going?" the women would have asked from the doorways if she had slowed down, even though they knew where she was going. She passed the little chapel at the top of the ridge, the last reminder of all she was leaving behind, and followed the switchbacks down to the river.

The river was higher today because of yesterday's rain, but she still bounced across it easily enough. The hard rocks of the river under her tires, she drove on, pushing aside the alarms her father had raised as well as the opinions of her neighbors, and focused on the slow uncoiling of the venomous serpent.

She climbed out of the riverbed and bumped up the road to the Pink House. Memo came out to meet her, Telegram at his side like a satrap. The Doberman had steadied under Memo's authority, no longer barking and leaping at the fence. Memo's face, bronzed by the sun, lit up in greeting.

"Perfect timing," he said, holding the door for her. "Outside, Telegram." The dog lay down on the veranda with practiced precision. They went into the living room and he closed the door. "I've just come from Huehue myself."

"You don't have a car."

"I don't need one. I have friends."

Sandra arched her brows. "Really? And I thought you were a recluse. Who are these friends?" Could he be seeing a woman? She knew so little about him. Unlike her husband, who was as safe and predictable as the academic calendar.

Memo moved closer to her. "No one you know."

"Why are you so mysterious?" She held his gaze and let it thrill her. She knew she was flirting. She smiled and let him see it. He lifted one furry eyebrow in response. She knew she was hurtling toward disaster. Her heart was banging out warning to her brain. She made herself stop thinking. The sense of duty that she'd worn like a hazmat suit all day lifted off, leaving her raw and ready for danger.

"It adds to my allure, don't you think?" His hands, those hands that had hypnotized her, on her shoulders now pulled her to him. Just before he kissed her she closed her eyes to feel his lips, hard, hot, sucking her into him. She kept her eyes closed, leaned into him and kissed him back, eating his lips, tasting salt and spice. She put her hands on his back and dug her fingers into his muscles through his shirt. They shuddered, sending a vibration through her to her inner thighs. She clung to sensation and banished thoughts of every man who had defined her to this point—father, husband, son were shucked, leaving only Memo. His hands stayed clamped to her shoulders until at last he pulled his mouth away. She opened her eyes, gasping for breath, and saw him staring at her with a slight smile. "Have we waited long enough?"

The two weeks they had waited, that had seemed interminable, vanished into history. This was what she'd waited for, this myopic present. She took in the closed door, not bolted but guarded by the sphinxlike Doberman, and the milky panes of the back windows letting in light but no prying eyes. No human eyes, but God's would see. Whether her father's vengeful God or her own more forgiving one, it wouldn't matter when the time came for her just deserts. She measured the distance through the kaleidoscopic rooms, the distance of her free-fall from grace. "No one can know about this," she said. She took his hand, an action that felt impossibly bold to her, and listened again to the heartbeat pounding in her ears. Now rather than warning, it sounded like drumroll. Anticipation. Memo's hand was surprisingly soft and smooth. He let her hold it, leaned over and kissed her neck close to her ear, just grazing her skin, sending another jolt of electricity through her core.

His mouth still close to her ear he said, "You can rely on my discretion." The words of a lawyer or a priest, belied when he slid his free hand up under her blouse and pulled one breast out of its cup. She let herself succumb to the pure sensation of his fingers twisting her nipple. She squeezed his hand to tell him *Go on, do it. Tame me, break me, whatever it takes.* Then she made herself stop forming words, always her enemy, always sounding like words from her father, the pastor, the priest, the police. If she could stop the words she could stop the rules. She let go of his hand so that he could use it to unhook her bra.

Over his shoulder she could see the blue bedroom. She pushed her hands into the waistband of his jeans and gripped his hipbones like a steering wheel, guiding him awkwardly backwards toward the bed. She kept her eyes open but unfocused, watching out only for the merest of directional signals. His tongue in her ear was communicating messages in a new language it took all of her attention to decipher. When his calves bumped up against the bed she pushed him onto it. He pulled her down with him, then rolled her over and looked down on her.

"I don't usually do this kind of thing," she said.

Again the twitch of his smile. "Don't I know it." He straddled her, unbuttoning her blouse.

He probably did do this kind of thing, all the time, she thought. "How can I trust you?" Even she knew that wasn't the right question, when all she wanted was to keep the thing uncoiling inside her from closing itself up again. She lifted her arms so he could pull the blouse over her head.

"I won't ever hurt you," he said. She looked him in the eye and saw that he was serious. Experimentally she reached for his fly and unzipped his jeans, amazed at her power. He lowered onto her, helping her wriggle out of her own jeans, helping her help him get naked on top of the covers. Her eyes closed as she felt his mouth on her breasts, on her stomach, sliding down. She listened not to words but to her heart beating and to the slow throbbing of rain on the tile roof overhead. She caught hold of the throbbing and rode it like a wave, not thinking, feeling it slip, recapturing it, not letting it go until it lifted her up to an anguished gasp and pleasure too sharp to bear. She pushed him away and pulled him back with her legs wrapped around him, guiding him in. She opened her eyes and watched the venom strike, arching him up and away from her. Sweat glistened on his forehead and the muscles of his arms and neck, the drumming of the rain crescendoed until she felt charged with control of the heavens' outpouring. Their two naked bodies swam in the blue room, surely not made one in any Biblical sense, but united as if in crime.

7

Several months later

SOMETHING WASN'T RIGHT. Fernando sensed it the minute he pulled into the carport. Sandra's car wasn't there. No Mozart ran yapping to meet him and bite his ankles. Even the birds in their cages were silent. No doves cooing, no parakeet mimicry, no canary tra-la-la's. "Anyone home?" he called. His voice echoed in the garden.

Tona came out of the kitchen wiping her hands on her apron. "Don Fernando, fíjese! The little dog was hit by a car. Doña Sandra took him to the vet. Omar went with her, crying and wailing to break your heart. She told Omar the doctor would fix little Mozart. But Don Fernando, I think she gives the child false hope."

"Oh dear." Fernando could care less about the wretched dog, but he couldn't bear the thought of his son's tears. Omar was too young to suffer his first loss. That was the trouble with pets.

"Walter and Leti are going to their grandmother's after school. I'll have your lunch ready in a minute."

"Thanks, Antonia. I'll be right down." He went upstairs to change his shoes and splash water on his face. In the bathroom mirror he saw a man who shouldn't have a care. He'd paid off the Rattlesnake. He would never have to grovel to that creepy lowlife again. Memo's project out at Sapoclok was proceeding, and Fernando visited regularly to consult on the construction, giving advice on the situation of the plant at the base of the pine knoll, the leveling of the land, the digging of the well. Fernando liked to build. The man in the mirror was a man of substance, an upstanding man in fine old Remedios. That thought caused him an inward chuckle. He heard a faint keening.

Keening?

He came out of the bathroom and followed the sound to the closed door of the boys' bedroom. He cracked the door open. The shutters were drawn and the room was dark. Clothes and books and papers were piled on the floor. A lump lay under the covers of a bed, curled into a fetal position. The crying was muffled by a pillow.

"Félix?" Fernando was bewildered. It had been years since he'd seen Félix cry. He remembered it with a stab of remorse, the three children on the sofa watching *The Wizard of Oz.* Sandra was out, and he'd put them in front of the TV while he worked. Félix was seven or eight and was supposed to be taking care of his younger siblings. Instead, tears were streaming silently down his face. The little ones were unaffected. Even then Félix should have been too old to cry. And now?

He went to the bed and pulled the covers back. Félix grabbed the pillow and held it tight over his head.

"Go away," he said.

"Félix," he said again, trying to get a grasp on what his heart was telling him was dire. "We'll get a new dog." He held his hand on his son's back. It shook with sobs. He stroked it, sitting awkwardly on the edge of the bed. Félix was the size of a man now, but Fernando wanted to hold him in his arms and protect him from all evil and hurt, even from death itself. He stroked and made soft sounds until the shaking ceased. Félix rolled over and sat up.

"It's not the dog," he said. He wiped his eyes with the pillow and leaned back against the wall, looking over his father's head as if not wanting to meet his gaze. "Gloria dumped me."

"I don't believe it! Why?" Sandra was right: the girl must be an idiot.

"She told me she's fallen in love with someone else, a friend of ours at school. I thought he was my friend. Now she's with him. We were together three years. My life is over, Papi."

"No it isn't, mijo." Fernando dug a handkerchief out of his pocket and thrust it at his son. "This happened to me when I was your age. My best friend took my girl." Well, actually Anita had never been Fernando's girl, but he'd felt as devastated at the time as if she were, and he'd lost not only a girl but also his best friend. "It will pass; you'll get over it."

Félix blew his nose, then clenched the handkerchief. "I don't think so. I can't study." He swept his hand around the room at the papers that sprawled like disaster victims. "I'm failing all my courses." It was September. Félix was supposed to graduate in a month.

"Don't worry. You can defer med school."

"I never sent in the applications. Even before Gloria left me, Papá, I didn't want to go to med school."

Fernando was stunned. Hadn't Sandra been on top of this, talking over schools with him, getting him ready? "But you like science. You're good at it." At least, better than he was at literary and social studies.

Félix hung his head and sighed. "It was your dream. I wanted to do it for you. But I can't. I'm no good at anything."

Fernando didn't know what to say. This new calamity had blindsided him. He didn't know where to direct his anger. At his son, for squandering his opportunities, at the girlfriend, for putting him into this state, at the Rattlesnake for distracting him when he should have been paying attention to his son, at Sandra…at the fates that never seemed to stop delivering bad news. Or at the fear that twisted his guts at seeing his son cry. "Félix. You shouldn't feel this way. No girl, no med school is worth this. Tell me what I can do." He reached out to enfold his boy in a comforting embrace.

Félix flung himself back onto the bed. "Nothing, Papi. Go away." He closed his eyes.

Fernando sat looking at him. His firstborn—in agony, and he was helpless. "Félix, let's talk about it."

The boy's eyes remained closed. Long minutes passed in silence. Fernando breathed deeply. "OK. Rest. We'll talk later." He stood up, looked around the dark and disordered room. Something had to be done. Sandra surely could handle this. It was her area of expertise, not his. He left.

Over his solitary lunch he tried to convince himself that Félix would come out fine. This was one of those adolescent traumas. He'd had his and had survived. Kids survived. Most of them. Recently a neighbor's boy had died. He'd been studying at the university in Guate. He'd fallen out of a high window. No one knew the facts. Rumors swirled. Maybe a girlfriend was involved. Maybe drugs. Maybe he fell or maybe he jumped. His parents said he fell. Who could bear to talk to them or say otherwise?

After lunch he tried to work in his home office, but he remained conscious of Félix in the upstairs room. Sandra was late. He had a headache. He couldn't concentrate. It was getting dark when Sandra finally arrived. The silent house exploded in noise. Three children emerged from the car and came toward him.

"Look, Papi!" Leti held a fur bundle wriggling in her arms. She lifted the dangling puppy up to him.

"What's that?" Fernando said.

"Our new dog! His name is Happy."

Sandra brought up the rear. "He's a Jack Russell terrier. The vet was selling him. The timing was right."

"I see. Mozart…?"

Sandra put a finger over her lips.

"Félix is in his room. I need to talk to you."

"It's been a long day. After they go to bed. Kids, let's get Happy his supper and make him a bed." She steered them past Fernando.

He was watching the evening news on TV when he heard the gate clang shut. Sandra appeared in the living room, her face pale and distraught. "Félix went out," she said. "You have to go after him."

"What?"

"You have to get him to come home. I'm so afraid of what he might do. Talk to him."

"I tried to talk to him. I tried to talk to *you*. What's going on?"

"Gloria left him. Three weeks ago. He's desperate. I've never seen him like this. Nothing I say makes any difference. Boys his age…" She broke off. Fernando wondered if she too was thinking about the neighbor's boy. "Go. Find him."

Fernando left the house and went out into the dark street, looking up and down for signs of where Félix might have gone. It wasn't late, but there were seldom people out on the streets of Remedios after dark. He headed toward the town square with no plan of how to find his son, feeling his futility. A café on the corner of the plaza was still open. He went in and asked two men having beans and coffee at a formica table and the girl who had served them, but no one had seen a young man roaming the streets. The arcade in front of the muni was vacant, and by the fountain he found only a couple of drunks sleeping on benches. The darkness and emptiness all around entered his soul. He stopped to watch the water fall out of the fountain into the catch basin, only to be recycled to the top, to fall and rise again and again. Falling and rising. All he wanted was to raise his family, provide for his children, care for his wife. Why had Sandra waited so long to tell him? Waited until crisis struck. He'd hardly seen Sandra these past few months; she was always busy coming and going. He felt unconnected to her. It was disorienting. He was losing his ballast. Was Félix in danger? He'd heard panic in Sandra's voice. She was always in charge, under control. *I've never seen him like this.* Félix wasn't the kind to go out of a high window. There weren't any in Remedios. There was only a high bridge over a ravine, in the mountains not far from the house. Could he have gone in that direction?

Footsteps in the distance penetrated Fernando's thoughts and he snapped to attention. He crossed the square and the street beyond it to the band shell, where he found a policeman he knew patrolling.

"Manuel! Good evening. How are you?"

"Don Fernando! What are you doing out at this hour?"

"Looking for my son. That kid! Can you believe it? He goes out for 'a walk' and he's got my car keys. I have to leave early in the morning. I need my keys! I can't be looking for him at six a.m. Have you seen him?"

"No. Where do you think he might have gone?"

Fernando didn't want to say, the bridge over the ravine. Nor did he want Manuel to leap to the conclusion that Félix was out of his father's control, meeting friends at this hour who could be up to no good, gang members possibly, because that was what happened to the sons of so many good families these days. "Probably his cousin's house, and he forgot the time. I'm on my way over there. I'll probably find them watching TV."

Manuel walked off satisfied and Fernando watched him go, wishing he could have asked for help. Now he had to walk up the road into the mountains toward the ravine. Part of him said it was crazy. It was night. His leather-soled shoes slipped on the steep pavement. Dogs barked as he passed the last houses in town. Past the last house and he had no flashlight. He'd been up this way in his car and it hadn't seemed far; it was much longer on foot, in the dark. The moon was out and its light was cold. The Cuchumatanes loomed up in a dark façade. The ravine dropped at his right into an abyss. The road turned to gravel. He panted with the exertion of the unaccustomed climb. Félix had always been a responsible child, eager to please. But sensitive to failure. The first time he'd received a failing mark for reading, he'd cried. Sandra had worked with him after school until he had passed. It had been a struggle. When he didn't get chosen for the first string, he quit the soccer team. He never went to see his younger brother play. Sandra had said, "Don't force him."

Should he have forced him or done something to toughen him? Instead, he'd done everything he could to soften life's blows and smooth Félix's path. Yes, he'd looked forward to having a son in med school, but mostly for Félix's sake. So that he would be secure, never have to borrow money from someone like the Rattlesnake. The ascent seemed to be taking forever. Around every corner he expected to come to the bridge. All he saw was a glimmer of faint lights from a few scattered houses at the head of the valley. He would have welcomed an oncoming car, but there was no traffic. He couldn't see down to the bottom of the ravine, lost in shadow. How could he not have seen this coming? How had he missed the signs of his son's despair?

He was sweating, although the night was cold. If med school was truly out of the picture, he'd have to come up with a new plan for Félix. Maybe send him to work for Pepe in Mexico. A change of scene. He tried to replace the image that kept coming to him of Félix on the bridge. Where *was* the bridge? Finally he came to it, a short one-lane span of cement with a low wall. There was nobody on it, no figure leaning against the wall in contemplation of ending his life. He walked to the center of the bridge and looked over the wall. Far below he could see a gleam of moonlight on water, and he could hear the roar of the water over rocks. There had been several suicides off the bridge in the twenty years since it had been built, and some talk of raising the wall higher. But that would have obstructed the view of opposing traffic, and nothing had ever been done. Fernando imagined the plunge from the wall, the rush of wind, the horrible pain of impact, and shuddered. He peered into the shadows below but couldn't see anything. He studied the forbidding sides of the ravine to see if it would be possible for him to clamber down for closer inspection. The phone in his pocket buzzed, startling him.

"Fernando." Sandra's voice spoke into his ear. "Elena just called. Félix is over there with Fredy. He's going to spend the night. I said it was OK."

Just as Fernando had predicted to Manuel. If he'd gone over to his sister's house as he'd said he was and waited, Félix would have shown up. Instead, he was standing out in the cold in the dark.

"Fernando. Did you hear me? Where are you?"

"The suicide bridge. Sandra, we have to talk. Why didn't you tell me Félix was in trouble?"

"I didn't want to worry you."

"You think today didn't worry me? My grown son crying like a small child! Finding out he's completely fucked up at school. That this has been going on for how long? Months? Sacred Virgin! What were you thinking?" There was no response, and he realized he'd lost the signal. He tried to call her back, but his phone refused to regain connection. Disgusted, he put it back in his pocket and began trudging back down the road. His feet hurt. By the time he reached home he had blisters. Sandra was waiting up for him in bed.

"I should have told you sooner," she said. "I was afraid you'd bawl him out. That would only make things worse."

Fernando got in under the covers next to her and lay back exhausted. "I'll have a talk with him tomorrow."

"Don't yell."

"I won't."

He left the house at six in the morning. That part of what he'd told Manuel was truth. He had a meeting in Xela. On the long drive to Guatemala's second city thoughts of Félix nagged him. He couldn't shake the sound of Félix weeping, the memory of sweat and cold on the bridge, the relief and anger that had washed over him when Sandra's call came. Was it selfishness for him to want a moment's peace? Instead he was battered by one calamity after the next. His focus returned during his meeting with colleagues from San Carlos-Quetzaltenango. They reviewed their latest joint project in political internships in rural villages throughout the western highlands and the work absorbed him, making him feel productive again. Satisfaction with the project lasted through the return drive. He'd be home in time for a late lunch, and he would take control of his domestic issues, starting with a talk with Félix. Determination buoyed him. On the road between Huehue and Remedios he pulled out his phone and called Félix, who answered on the second ring. A hopeful sign; his phone was on.

"Mijo. I want to have a chat with you. Relaxed. No pressure. Are you at home?"

"I'm at the Pink House, Papá, with Tío Memo. Can you come out? We have an idea I want to discuss with you."

Tío Memo? When had the kids started calling Memo uncle? It was only natural, Fernando supposed. They'd taken to spending Sundays out at the country place again, and Memo had made them welcome. "I'm on my way," he told Félix. He wouldn't stop at home first. He was too anxious to get to Félix. The boy had suffered a blow; Fernando would boost his confidence and make him realize he still had plenty of options. More than his father did at that age! But what on earth could he be discussing with Memo?

September had been drier than usual. He crossed the river and drove up past the cornfields. The corn was high, obscuring any signs of new construction. He pulled into the Pink House. Memo and Félix met him on the veranda and Memo invited him inside. Fernando noticed a sparkle in his son's eyes and an eagerness in his step, trotting after Memo like a puppy. Something had changed.

"Come into the dining room. My new table and chairs came," Memo said. He had told Fernando he wanted to spruce the place up, and it needed it, God knew. "Félix, fetch your papi a beer."

The table was mahogany, more elegant than Fernando had been expecting for a country house, with eight matching chairs. Fernando was afraid to put his beer bottle down on the gleaming wood, but after he'd had a chance to admire it, Memo covered it with a large plain tablecloth. "I have some chicken. Félix and I already ate but if you came straight from Xela you must be hungry."

Fernando waited until Memo brought him a plate of chicken and rice and a basket of tortillas to ask, "So Félix, what's this idea of yours?"

"It's brilliant! Tío Memo needs a chemist to supervise his plant. He's offered to send me to Mexico to finish my studies and train for the job."

Fernando placed his drumstick on his plate, wiped his fingers, and stared at Memo aghast. He didn't know where to begin. The thought occurred to him that Memo was bent on revenge after all, that this was somehow a plot to destroy the Granados family. Before he could speak Memo spread his hands. "Félix came to me this morning with his proposal. At first, like you, I didn't think it was a good idea. I didn't want to involve your son in the business. He's young. But, like his father, he's very persuasive—and smart. He had figured out what the product is."

Fernando couldn't believe his ears. "How?"

"Apparently after our initial conversation about the factory you did an Internet search on the product. You left a trail of websites on your computer, and Félix happened upon it.

When he heard you discussing the plant with your brothers, he put two and two together. You might want to put some password protection on your computer."

"He has it, Tío. I know the password. But don't worry, Papá. I'm the only one who knows about the meth."

"He assures me he's been most discreet."

"I can't allow this. It's out of the question. Félix is a *boy*, Memo. Seventeen."

"At his age, I was inducted into the army." Did Fernando detect a subtle dig? "But I understand your concern. I appreciate it. I shared it. However, when Félix came to me he was very…upset. He told me a bit about his recent heartbreak and despondency over his career prospects. We talked over his problems at school and I drew him out a little. He revealed his love of labwork and his curiosity about how things work. He doesn't thrive in the school setting. He needs a more…practical environment for learning. I can provide that in Veracruz."

"Veracruz?"

"In a very advanced laboratory where he can train hands-on. I think he'll pick it up quickly. Like a sponge!"

"It's too dangerous. These labs blow up all the time." Fernando hadn't revealed to Memo how much he knew about meth labs before. He didn't want to venture onto Memo's turf. But now it was his flesh and blood at risk.

"They blow up when they're run by amateurs, Papi. I've done a lot of research—and I've covered my tracks on the Internet." Félix glanced at Memo. "We're going to run a safe lab. It can be done."

"That's only one of the dangers. There's…law enforcement for example." And working for a brutal cartel, for another, but Fernando couldn't say that to Memo's face. They had never discussed Memo's Mexican connections or named a cartel. Fernando had stopped eating, but he took a large sip of beer.

"Crystal meth is not even on their radar screen," Félix said. "They're looking for marijuana, cocaine, heroin. All they know about meth is a few guys who cook out of barrels in the backs of their pickup trucks. They won't be looking for a factory."

Do you know what this stuff does to people? Fernando wanted to ask. As if he'd read his thoughts Félix said, "No one here uses it. It's going far away. We won't have anything to do with that. Tío Memo will take care of it." Again a sidelong glance at Memo.

"Keeping it in the family, as it were," Memo said, choosing his words delicately it seemed, "has great security advantages. We all share in the same…aspirations."

No, Fernando thought. *No, no, no!*

"You're not eating your lunch," Memo observed. "Félix, step outside for a few minutes. Let me talk to your father alone." Now it was toward his father that Félix directed a look, this time a beseeching one. He got up and left, closing the dining room door behind him.

"Fernando. You can trust me. I know the boy has given you a scare. He didn't tell me too much, but I extrapolated. I'll take care of him as if he were my son. This will be good for him. He needs a sense of purpose, some *self-esteem* as the Americans say." He said the words in English. Fernando didn't know much English, but he'd heard that phrase.

He shook his head, feeling defeat creep in. "Last night, I actually went up to the suicide bridge. I thought Félix might jump."

"I know."

How did Memo know? Did Félix know? The thought alarmed Fernando. Could a father's fear turn into a suggestion to a troubled mind? "Nothing can happen to my son. Understand?"

"Nothing will." He made it sound like a statement and a promise.

"What can I tell Sandra? She'll never agree."

"She'll agree. You're going to get Félix out of town for a while, get him away from his troubles. I know you can convince her."

Fernando was not so sure. "She has a mind of her own."

"She relies on your judgment. The study of chemistry will fascinate Félix, you'll tell her, and take his mind off the girl."

"The chemistry of cleaning supplies?" Fernando asked. That *was* their cover, wasn't it?

"Ecological soaps, detergents, and cleaning compounds," Memo said. "It's a very modern science."

Fernando sighed. This could be his best option for his son. It could be his only option. "I'll give it a shot," he said.

8

2013

MEMO GLOWERED AT HIS COMPUTER SCREEN. The numbers were still bad. The pressures to move product were building. He was tired of whiny emails from F-40 complaining of the delays. Let the Mexicans try and build a meth operation in Guatemala. He'd agreed to this assignment as a favor to them, although they didn't know it. They thought they were compensating him for what the Gulf Cartel had done to his family. As if Huehuetenango were a territory of value to anyone but a half-breed orphan chingado Guatemalteco bastard. He let his frown fade and shook his head. It didn't make sense to lose his temper. His modus operandi was all about control, and he'd kept that through the tedious months of construction setbacks and mountain-moving efforts to get a state-of-the-art super-lab running in the land of mañana. They'd been up for two months. He closed the spreadsheet and opened up his mail.

And found it was logged into Geraldo's account. What the fuck? The bodyguard was another problem. The Mexicans had sent Geraldo down to work for Memo, but also, Memo knew, to keep an eye on him. Now it looked as if he'd been snooping in Memo's computer. Memo valued his privacy. His annoyance with the Mexicans flared from ember to flame. It was time he sent them a message that he was in charge of Huehue. If he wanted a bodyguard, he would hire his own. A knock came at his office door. He closed his mail and shut down his fury.

Félix entered. "What's up?" Memo asked.

"The shipment of monometh didn't come in. I called the Pirate down in Port Q. There was a sting operation last night. PNC, army, DEA, the works. They took 320 barrels of chemical and the ship captain, Chinese guy I think, into custody. We can't cook."

"*Process*," Memo corrected him. "We don't *cook* here. That's something you do in the back of a pickup." He closed his computer. More delay. "We have a delivery scheduled for next week. How much product do you have ready to go?"

"Almost 950 pounds."

That was pretty good, Memo thought, for six peasants and one high school dropout in their first two months on the job. Bringing Félix into the business had cemented his relations with the Granados family. Not that they needed much cement. Fernando treated him like a brother, and Sandra had been his off and on secret mistress for a year. Memo enjoyed complexity. As for Félix, he was a good kid. His talent for chemistry had flourished in Veracruz and under Memo's mentorship. "So we need methylamine right now," Memo said, "to stay on schedule."

"Do you have another source?" In addition to the chemistry, Félix appreciated the business aspect and was eager to learn the ropes.

"I don't need another source. The Pirate is just an errand boy. You have to go over his head." Memo flipped open his phone and tapped keys. "The DEA." He waited while the phone rang the fifteen rings Karl used to fend off unwanted calls. Karl himself answered. "Hombre," Memo said, "Curly

here. I have a problem down in Port Q. I need my 320 barrels of Ivory Liquid or ladies all over my department aren't
going to be able to do their laundry." Memo looked at Félix
and smiled. He let Karl retell the sting operation and add a
bunch of excuses, then cut in. "I don't care how many sen-
ators you've got looking over your shoulder. I gave you the
Patriarch; now get me my detergent." He nodded his head
and reeled a finger in rhythm as Karl spun out his explanation of what was involved in fulfilling Memo's request. Finally,
because they were both busy men he said, "That's enough. I
get it. It's a pleasure doing business with you, my friend." He
snapped his phone shut.

"We'll pick it up tomorrow. Our friends at the PNC are
keeping it safe," he said, using the common acronym for the
national police.

"It's as easy as that?" Félix was looking on with admiration.

"It's not easy," Memo said. "I've spent years cultivating
relationships. Karl I got to know when I was training with the
FBI in Quantico. The US is very generous with its counterter-
rorism training. Americans are easy to get along with. They
divide the world into good guys and bad guys. You take out
one or two of their bad guys, and you're on their team." He
got up from his desk and put an arm around Félix's shoulders.
"Let's get Geraldo to run you back to the factory. In this rain
you can drown between your front door and the crapper."

Not that Memo had an outhouse. The Pink House, while
remaining unchanged from the outside, had undergone signif-
icant improvements inside. Its walls were now a tasteful white,
its floors terracotta tile, its furnishings leather and tropical
hardwoods, and its marble bathroom featured a Jacuzzi and
sauna. Memo walked Félix to his office door and out onto the

veranda. Sheets of water fell in the yard. "Our biggest problem isn't the national police. It's that frigging river road." The river had been impossible to cross since the rainy season began. "I'm going to have to build a real road. In fact, I think it's time Huehue got a ring road. That will be our project next year."

"You're going to build a highway, Tío?"

"Hearts and minds, Félix. You give people jobs and services and you never have to worry. Go see if Geraldo's in the kitchen." He watched Félix trot down the veranda. In fact, Memo never stopped worrying. He'd seen too many transfers of power—from army to politicos, local dealers to international cartels—to trust anyone's allegiance. Returning to Remedios had stirred up memories of the one time in his life he'd felt safe, when he'd played soccer and gone to school like any middle-class boy.

Félix and Geraldo came out of the kitchen toward him. Geraldo. One thing that set Memo apart from others in his trade was that he didn't enjoy violence for its own sake. He preferred to use intelligence and diplomacy. But he wouldn't rule out the use of force when it was required. They joined him to stride toward the end of the veranda where he'd added a carport. "Geraldo, we're dropping Félix at the factory and heading into town."

The three of them got into the Land Cruiser, Geraldo at the wheel. The gate opened electronically now, and they pulled out into the muddy lane and drove past a cornfield to the plant entrance. Ringed by chain-link fence, the factory was a low cement structure in a sea of mud. Not quite an industrial park, but serviceable. It looked like the warehouse it was purported to be. They dropped off Félix and continued on down the horrible river road toward Huehue.

Waiters greeted Memo in the indoor dining room at Casa Real, where Fernando was already ensconced at a table by the fireplace. "Sit down and let the fire take the chill off!" Fernando said. "I've ordered a bottle of Cabernet. How are things?" They met for lunch once a week and Memo kept Fernando up to date on what he needed to know. Fernando was nervous about the business and didn't want to know too much. Memo struck a tightrope walker's balance.

"Good." The waiter came and poured their wine. They put in their orders without having to look at the menu. Memo ordered steak; Fernando, who was watching his cholesterol, grilled shrimp.

Fernando started. "My cousin, the one with the greenhouse down below the property, has been breaking my balls recently. He says our truck traffic is tearing up the road. He claims foul odors are coming out of the warehouse at night. He threatens to go to the municipality with a complaint."

"Hmmm. What did you tell him?"

"That we had trash left over from the construction that we had to burn. Maybe we should put in some kind of air filtration."

"We have a system, very sophisticated, but occasional leakage is inevitable. Come out with me after lunch. You haven't seen the lab since it was finished. You'll be impressed." Memo watched Fernando's eyes widen, saw the worry lines on his forehead. Fernando had come out frequently during construction, maintaining a proprietary concern over the land, but had stayed away since operation began. Memo knew his misgivings and decided that it was past time to overcome them. He wanted Fernando deeply involved, invested in the project's success. "Don't worry about your cousin. I have a friend who can give him a call if he causes trouble." He told Fernando about his road building plans. "That should keep him happy for a while."

"If the neighbors don't put up a stink. Every time you go to build a road around here, some group decides it's going through their town center or favorite pinewoods and fights to stop it. People don't like progress."

"You can't stop progress," Memo said.

"I'll drink to that." Fernando clinked his glass. His phone buzzed. "Not even for long enough to eat lunch." He answered it. "Yes, my love…. He's right here…. I'll ask him. I'll be late tonight. There's a meeting after my evening class…. Yes, my sweet." He hung up. "That was Sandra."

Memo's lips twitched. "I guessed."

"Her sister, the one who's a lawyer in Xela, is coming for the weekend. It's their father's birthday. We're having a small party on Saturday. She wants me to invite you."

Sandra was brazen about including him in family gatherings. Memo didn't know who among Fernando's family and neighbors had guessed their relationship, but of one thing he was certain: Fernando himself knew nothing. He was as blind to his wife's secret life as he was to any of her faults. Memo had been subtly encouraging him to try a fling with one of his students—there was one girl he talked about, smart like a fox, who'd been giving him the eye—but Fernando would have none of it. "When you have a tigress in the lair, why look elsewhere for a kitten, eh?" he'd kidded Fernando, trying to draw him out, but Nando had only given him a look. He wouldn't talk with Memo about his sex life. From Sandra, Memo knew it wasn't so hot. "I'm honored," he said.

"Does it bother you? That my father-in-law is a cop?"

"Not at all." Memo dug into the steak the waiter had delivered quietly before retreating to a respectful distance. "I enjoy having good relations with the police. Especially an incorruptible officer like Don Alejandro."

"He gives me a pain in the liver, but I have to put up with him."

Fernando nattered on about family and university gossip while they finished lunch, which Memo had the waiter put on his tab. They went out to the courtyard parking area, where Geraldo waited in the Land Cruiser. "Meet me out at the plant," he told the bodyguard. "I'm riding out with Don Fernando." He put a subtle emphasis on the title, to indicate to Geraldo that the bodyguard's position was that of a servant.

"I don't think that's a good idea, boss. With the river high..." Geraldo looked Fernando up and down, as if it were his presence Geraldo distrusted rather than the river.

"You're not paid to tell me what you think. I'll thank you to do what I say." Memo turned his back on the Land Rover, got into the passenger seat of Fernando's SUV, and slammed the door. "Let him go first," he told Fernando. "I don't need his eyes on my back."

They drove out of Huehue and back toward Remedios in heavy rain. Memo watched the windshield wipers and pondered what to do about Geraldo. They reached the outskirts of Remedios and turned off by the soccer field, which lay green, sodden, and empty under the rain. The soccer field where he'd first met Fernando. "Those were the days, eh Nando?" Memo said.

Fernando kept the SUV's tires in the muddy track that skirted the field and followed the edge of the river upstream. "The good old days, you mean?"

"Exactly." Memo folded his hands in his lap, at ease despite the jouncing of the vehicle. "Whatever happened to Anita Carillo?" He'd never brought up the subject of his high-school girlfriend, and had watched Fernando skirt around the painful memory several times in the past year.

Fernando jerked the steering wheel. "Her family moved to Guate during the Violence. I lost track of her."

"You dog. You were jealous, as I recall. Bet you planned that night at the guerrilla meeting." He watched Fernando stiffen, and chuckled. He didn't know exactly what Fernando had been thinking would happen that long-ago night, but his barb had clearly touched its mark. "I don't blame you. Anyway, joining the army worked out well for me."

"I'm glad of that." And Memo could see he was. It felt good to let his old friend off the hook. He'd kept Fernando dangling for a long time; it gave him power. He hadn't been sure he could count on Fernando's loyalty to their boyhood friendship when he had come back to Remedios. Fernando's welcome had been genuine. Fernando was openhearted. It was a quality that had gotten him into trouble, and would again, Memo suspected. But it was a quality that Memo envied. He'd never had the luxury, except for those few high-school years.

The river roared past them, foaming and brown, but the track was well above it on the gravel bank. There were no houses along this approach, and no other traffic, just the deep ruts from the trucks that had passed on their way to the plant. Geraldo had left the gate open where the road climbed up from the river. Fernando pulled into the factory entrance and parked in the shuttered loading dock. A sign over a small metal door read "Granados Eco-Clean." Memo pressed a button next to the door and looked up into the camera hidden in an overhead beam. The door opened and Geraldo let them into a large, dimly lit space where large barrels were stacked in aisles floor to ceiling.

"Félix knows that his papi's here?" Memo asked Geraldo, who nodded. "Good. Wait for us." He led Fernando deeper into the cavernous warehouse and gestured left and right. "The barrels are all coded so that we know what's inside—precursor or product. We have thirty different chemicals in here. It's important to keep them straight."

They passed two workers in white coveralls moving sacks of what could have been cement or fertilizer off a forklift onto shelves and came to another metal door. Next to it hung a row of coveralls and masks. "The lab is sealed off. But today you won't need a mask." He took a key out of his pocket and fitted it to the door and punched in a code. He opened the door and then stepped aside to let Fernando appreciate the contrast. Bright light gleamed on a row of shiny steel cauldrons topped by glass domes, connected by wires and tubes to tanks and control panels with rows of switches, dials, and red and green lights. Félix shuffled toward them pushing the hood of his coverall back, his slippered feet gliding over the polished tile floor.

"What do you think, Papá?" His face glowed like the lab.

Fernando looked around with wide eyes. "Very modern. You know how to work all these machines?" he asked Félix. In his voice Memo detected not just incredulity but also pride. He'd deliberately brought Fernando on a day when it would be the machinery and not the bubbling, fuming product that was evident. The product scared Fernando, Memo knew that.

"Your son is a first-rate chemist, Fernando," Memo said. Pride would win Fernando over, conquering his fear.

"Right now we're drying and finishing off yesterday's run." Félix pointed at racks of trays in an illuminated glass and steel box. Fernando stared at the sheets of glasslike material in the trays.

"Notice the ventilation system," Memo said. Large ducts lined the ceiling. "Everything is filtered. Safety is our number-one concern."

Fernando looked up and around. "You promised me I'd be impressed. It's quite something. No doubt about it." Memo noticed that he touched nothing, and gave the shelves of bottles and flasks a wide berth. That was fine; it showed a healthy respect. Fernando looked at his watch. "Thanks for the tour. Time for me to get back to the university."

Memo escorted him out to his car. The rain had stopped, but the ground was still muddy beyond the roofed-over loading bay. He slapped Fernando on the back. "Go educate the youth." He watched the SUV pull out and make its way slowly toward the river, then turned to Geraldo, who stood waiting for orders. "Run me up to the house."

He'd made up his mind.

Last year, the body of a local drug dealer had been found at the Green Lagoon, punctured by forty stab wounds. The dealer, a kid from the other side of Huehue, still had several bags of marijuana in his backpack. The police had decided it was a turf war. It seemed like a good place to take care of his Geraldo problem. The Mexicans would get the message.

They pulled through the electronic gate and under the carport. Telegram came trotting up the veranda straight for Geraldo, who pulled a rock out of his pocket and held it up in a threat. "Keep off me, you brute," he hissed at the Doberman. He always kept a rock ready, and Telegram seemed to enjoy goading him. Trust the Mexicans to send a bodyguard who was afraid of dogs. And couldn't remember to log off when he was spying on his employer. Memo took the Berretta M9 out of his shoulder holster and held it on Geraldo.

"Just keep the rock up there, boy. I'm taking your gun." He reached under Geraldo's jacket before the bodyguard had time to figure out what was happening.

"Boss, what's up?" Geraldo exclaimed. "I'm not going to hurt the dog."

"No," Memo agreed. "You're not. You're going for a walk in the woods." He tied Geraldo's hands behind him so that he could change into his country clothes and boots and pick up a small shoulder bag. Then he made the bodyguard walk in front of him, out the back gate, leaving Telegram inside. The Mexican struggled up the slippery trail until Memo untied his hands. He rubbed his wrists and looked at Memo suspiciously.

"Do you know what you're doing?" he asked.

"Yes," said Memo.

They clambered over the pine ridge, down the ravine and up the other side. Geraldo's city shoes slid out from under him several times, and he was covered in mud. The footing got easier as they went on through the woods toward the Green Lagoon. Pine needles covered the forest floor. Water dripped off the trees and ran down Memo's rain shell. Geraldo was soaked. They walked in silence. Memo could hear Geraldo's hoarse breath panting. When they got to the pond Memo made Geraldo stand at its edge facing the water, brown from the rain. "Don't take this personally," he said.

By now Geraldo had figured out his intentions. "You'll never get away with it," he said. "F-40 will finish you off."

Memo didn't answer. The only answer would have been that Geraldo wasn't that important. Instead, standing behind

Geraldo and still holding the Berretta in one hand, he took his garrote out of the shoulder bag. In a swift move he stowed the gun in the bag, looped the garrote over Geraldo's head, and pulled the wire taut around his neck with a sharp tug on the wooden handles. Geraldo threw out his arms, gurgled, and convulsed, twitching violently. Memo kept the pressure tight until he fell. Then he rolled him into the pond and watched him sink into the murky water and disappear.

He stowed his equipment and walked briskly back through the woods. By the time he reached the Pink House, he was sweating from the exertion. He stripped off his muddy clothes and got into the shower. He let it steam up the room and relax his muscles. Sandra would be coming in an hour, and he wanted to be ready.

9

June 8

FERNANDO FOUND HIS BROTHER EDGAR wedged awkwardly inside the dovecote in the courtyard patio. The doves, two white doves that were Sandra's most recent acquisitions, perched in the top of the cage, looking down on the invader. The birds quivered with anxiety. "What are you up to?" Fernando asked Edgar.

"Cleaning up the mess. The female keeps laying her eggs on the shelf by their food dish. They roll off the shelf and break."

Sure enough, Fernando could see the ruins of the tiny egg splatted on the bottom of the cage. Edgar wiped it up in old newspaper and extricated himself from the wire enclosure. "Maybe you should move the food dish down to the floor," Fernando suggested.

"No. They won't feed down there. Sandra's mother is bringing over a nest she uses for breeding this afternoon." Edgar's back was to the dovecote, the cage door standing ajar. His brother had a tendency toward absentmindedness. One dove swooped down and out of the cage, skimming Edgar's shoulder. He dropped the crumpled newspaper, made a grab for the bird, and missed.

"Now you're in trouble," Fernando said, watching the dove fly up to the edge of the tile roof overhanging the kitchen door, where it landed.

"Tona, fetch a broom!" Edgar called. "Get a towel!" Walter, coming downstairs in his soccer uniform, heard the ruckus, ducked into the bathroom and dashed into the courtyard with a towel. Tona came out of the kitchen and waved the broom at the dove, which fluttered off the roof and circled over their heads. Edgar took the towel and attempted to throw it over the bird. He missed. Sandra appeared in the courtyard. "What happened?" she asked Fernando, her voice tense to his ears.

"Edgar let your dove escape," he said, to make it clear the situation was not his fault.

"Help him catch her!" she ordered sharply. Not even Sandra, he thought, could really tell the male from the female. They were identical, both pure white, of equal size. She must have made an assumption.

The family ran around the courtyard dodging flower beds and furniture while the dove gyrated over them in confusion, as if she couldn't make her mind up whether she wanted freedom or capture. The dog joined in the chase, yapping frenetically. Fernando darted this way and that, feeling ineffectual in his attempts, angry at Edgar for getting him into this. What if the damned bird got away? Sandra would be devastated.

Walter chased the dove toward Fernando. He lunged toward her, missed, and banged his foot into the garden curb. "Ouch! Damn!" he shouted. The bird flew up over the kitchen roof and continued on up into the sky. His heart plummeted. He'd scared her off.

"Edgar, what do we do now?" Sandra cried out.

His brother stood looking after the receding dove, seeming unperturbed. "She'll be back. She knows where home is."

He was right. A few more spirals and the dove seemed to give up on freedom and circled back down toward Edgar. He tossed the towel again. This time it caught the dove and he brought her down. He reached inside the towel and grasped the dove, wrapping his hand expertly around her wings and holding them against her excited little body. Sandra came over and took the dove from Edgar. "There there," she said. "You're OK." She stroked the feathered head with a finger, placed the dove inside the dovecote, and firmly closed and bolted the door.

"Where's Félix?" Fernando asked her.

"In his room. Asleep. He got in around five this morning. Don't wake him," Sandra said. "He'll be up in time for the party." It didn't bother her that their son had been out at the plant all night working. She had no idea of what they were making out there. If she were to find out, he couldn't imagine what kind of hell would break loose. Since his visit to the lab he couldn't get the sight of Félix surrounded by boilers and tubes out of his mind. The visit had brought it home—the danger of explosion, according to what he'd seen on the Internet, the constant danger of discovery. There'd be no way for Félix to claim ignorance. Granted, the job had lifted Félix out of his depression. It had also elevated Memo to hero status in the boy's eyes. Fernando felt twinges of jealousy mixing with huge waves of anxiety. How had he gotten them all into this?

"Fernando," Sandra said.

He must have missed something. "I'm sorry, what did you say?"

"Can you drop Walter off for soccer practice on your way to the university?" Just fourteen, Walter had shot up in the last year to be a tall and lanky athlete, in contrast to his older brother. It was a relief to have one son he didn't have to worry about.

"Are you ready to go?" he asked Walter. "I'm leaving right now."

Because of the dove incident, he was late for his Saturday class. He gave a lecture on post-conflict economic theory in

Central America, a subject he knew so thoroughly he didn't have to prepare. He could spin off on tangents, create analogies, ask questions, start arguments, and bring the class back to the main theme. It restored his confidence, doing what he did well, and his mood improved. He didn't linger after class to confer with students and colleagues, but hurried back to Remedios for his father-in-law's birthday celebration. The sun was still out and the sky cloudless when he got home. The household hummed with preparations. Sandra was in the kitchen overseeing the preparation of tamales, salads, atole, snacks, and sauces with Tona and a muchacha. Leti and Walter set the long tables in the covered veranda that surrounded the garden on three sides. Luis had come from the ranch he was managing in Mexico bringing fresh mutton and was manning the grill. Fernando joined Luis at the grill and put his worries aside. The sun would shine, the guests would arrive, and the party would move forward under its own momentum.

At noon on the dot, Sandra's father, mother, and sister arrived at the gate. Fernando let them in, shooing away the barking dog. Happy was as excitable as his predecessor. "Don Alejandro!" He clasped his father-in-law's shoulders, towering over the wiry man and crushing him in a quick embrace. "Always punctual, always welcome! Congratulations on not looking a day over forty!" In fact, he was turning fifty-nine and nearing retirement, although Fernando couldn't imagine the hyperactive captain giving up police work.

"How was the drive from Xela?" he asked Sandra's sister Carolina.

"Uneventful." The new highway had shortened the trip to something under three hours, if you didn't get stuck behind a slow-moving truck on the blind curves and mountain passes. "I'm taking Mami and Papi back with me tonight."

"Having a holiday?" he asked his father-in-law.

"I'm going for work. Eight police were massacred last night in Salcajá, a substation outside Xela. Drug-traffickers from Huehuetenango are suspected. We're helping with the investigation." Don Alejandro rubbed his hands together with relish. "It looks to me like the Fuerzas."

Fernando tried to keep his voice neutral and disguise a renewed stab of anxiety. "What makes you think so?"

Don Alejandro gave a short laugh. "It was a particularly nasty piece of work. The policemen weren't only shot; they were also chopped up and their body parts scattered around the precinct. We think it's a revenge killing. And the chief of police is missing—either kidnapped or an accomplice."

"They think the whole precinct was running drugs," Carolina added.

"I wish Alejandro would send a younger officer to Xela. These narcos are animals," Doña Lidia said with a shudder. "But let's not talk about it right now." Omar bounded across the garden toward his grandmother.

"Come on in and have a glass of wine," Fernando said, leading his in-laws to a table and pulling a chair out for Doña Lidia. Sandra came out to offer her parents plates of fruit while Fernando popped a cork and started pouring Prosecco. Don Alejandro took his reluctantly. "To a man who is against pleasure on principle!" Fernando clinked his glass. His normal demeanor toward the older man was gentle kidding but with respect. "And yet you've enjoyed fifty-nine years of divine blessings."

Omar established himself in his grandmother's lap while Walter and Leti hung by her side, competing for attention.

Fernando kept refilling glasses as the patio filled up with guests. Elena and Vicente, the sister and brother who lived nearby, came with their families. Emilia, his sister who lived in San Cristóbal, arrived with her amiable husband Delfino. The Mexican and Guatemalan branches of the Granados family traveled back and forth almost every month. Nieces and nephews gathered around the grill. Félix emerged sleepily from his room and dutifully kissed both grandparents on the cheek. Fernando gave his son a glass of wine. "How's work in the stinking detergent factory?" Don Alejandro asked his grandson. Fernando's hand on his own glass shook.

"Not just detergent, Abuelito. We distribute all varieties of cleaning supplies—disinfectants, degreasers, drain cleaners, rust and lime removers, sweeping compounds, you name it." Fernando was amazed at his son's smooth lies. What else could Félix do? And what would happen if Don Alejandro took it into his head to inspect the plant? He downed his glass of Prosecco and poured himself another. The doorbell rang and he went to meet Memo at the gate.

"Just in time!" he greeted Memo. "The meat's coming off the grill. Hurry before the youngsters get it all. Do you want to invite your driver in?"

"I drove myself," Memo said.

"Unreliable help, huh?"

"You could say."

Sandra rose from her seat next to her father and turned her cheek so that Memo could brush it with his lips. There was assurance in the gesture. Fernando felt another pang of jealousy. Sandra's friendliness toward Memo, which he accepted as if it were his due, was one more sign the man had ingratiated himself into the family, on a par with Fernando's brothers in

Sandra's eyes. Greetings were exchanged, plates were loaded with food, people sat down to eat, Fernando, Memo, Luis, and Sandra at the table with her parents and sister. The children were with their cousins and aunt and uncles at another.

"Excellent mutton, Luis!" Fernando threw himself into his familiar role as host. Indeed, the meat was juicy and flavorful, if a bit tough. "My brother is quite the agronomist, Memo. The proof is in the tasting."

"You make it sound fancy. I'm a farmer," Luis protested. "Hot dirty work in the sun. But I like it better than sitting in an office."

"I know what you mean," Don Alejandro said. "My wife wants me to give up investigation for a desk job. That would kill me."

"If the Fuerzas don't kill you first," Fernando said. It was the wine talking, he knew. Memo raised an eyebrow. "My father-in-law is off to Xela to hunt for bad guys. Another massacre." He blundered on, hoping that speaking openly would appear more natural than silence on a subject on everyone's minds. "Like the one last year in the Petén. This time it's cops instead of plantation workers getting hacked up."

"Be careful, Don Alejandro," Memo said. "I found out when I lived in Mexico how dangerous these men are."

"They don't scare me." Don Alejandro's face flushed red. "Paul may have preached 'Return evil with good' and 'Turn the other cheek.' But these times call for Leviticus: 'Fracture for fracture, eye for eye, tooth for tooth, hand for hand, foot for foot!'" His speech was a little slurred and Fernando could tell he also was getting drunk. "That's the way to deal with narcotraffickers. Exterminate them like the vermin they are."

"Are you making rat poison out in that plant of yours, Memo?" Luis asked. His idea of a joke, no doubt. Fernando had kept his brothers ignorant of the true product of the factory. Only he and Félix knew.

Memo shook his head. "Just cleaning supplies. Nothing toxic." He gave Fernando a level look. It felt to Fernando like a warning that the conversation was getting too loose.

"Sandra, is there coffee?" he asked.

"Of course. But first the kids want Papá in the living room. Edgar strung up a piñata for him."

Omar had appeared at his grandmother's side again. "Abuelita! Abuelita!"

Carolina stood up. "Come along, Papi, let's sober you up." She took his arm and they followed the excited children.

"Time to party," Fernando said to Memo. "The old man doesn't usually drink."

"Isn't it against his religion?" Memo asked.

"As a general rule." They joined the surge as the gravitation of the party shifted. The living room furniture had been pushed back against the walls and the piñata hung from the ceiling fixture in the center of the room. It was an enormous clown head, round and white, with brilliant orange paper curls exploding from where its ears would have been, a bulbous orange nose, and large red lips. It rotated slowly on its cord, leering over the crowd. Félix had his grandfather's arm, steering him through the partiers.

"Blindfold him!" Walter shouted. The children laughed as Félix bent down to tie the handkerchief around Don Alejandro's eyes and spin him around. Walter put a stick in his hand. He made a few useless jabs into the air. Walter hooted.

Félix took his grandfather's arm and batted it toward the piñata so that the stick made contact. Don Alejandro grasped the stick in both hands and flailed wildly at the piñata. "Get it! Get it, Abuelito!" the children egged him on. Suddenly he was striking savagely, the piñata swinging over the children's heads. Blow after blow, putting his whole upper body into the fight. The stick caught the string that suspended the piñata and tore it from the ceiling fixture, sending it flying into the crowd. There was a shriek and a crash, and the kids were scrambling over the broken remains for the candies and treasures it spilled. Don Alejandro dropped the stick and yanked the handkerchief off.

10

June 14

FERNANDO FIRST NOTICED THE STRANGER loitering by the municipal building. He had long, pale hair hanging to his shoulders, a sharp jaw, pronounced, almost clownish lips, and a broad-brimmed floppy leather hat. He wore pitch-dark aviator sunglasses as if he were in disguise. A young man came out of the building and the stranger moved in on him. Fernando could see them talk briefly, then the stranger walked away and disappeared around the corner.

Fernando walked purposefully toward the muni, as if he had business there. He made a show of seeing the youth. He'd just placed him, a kid who had gone to school with Félix, Juan Maldenado. "What's up, Juanito? How's your old man?"

"Fine, Don Fernando. They're all good."

"Odd looking character you were just talking to," Fernando said. "What did he want?"

"He was looking for a Mexican name of Geraldo Lopez. Isn't he the guy who works for Don Memo out at Sapoclok?"

"There's a Geraldo out there," Fernando said with a sinking feeling. It wasn't surprising that all of Remedios knew who was living in the Pink House. He had kept a sharp ear out, however, and was fairly sure that so far no one knew what was being manufactured at Granados Eco-Clean. "Don't know his last name. What did you tell him?"

"Nothing. I asked who he was. I didn't like his looks."

"Who was he, did he say?"

"He said Geraldo was his cousin, that's all. His accent was Mexican."

Fernando began to feel like he was showing too much interest in the stranger, so he changed the subject. "We haven't seen you in a while. What are you up to these days?" He searched his memory. For all he knew Félix had cut Juan off after his breakup, as he had so many of his friends.

"I'm studying business and working as a tour guide in Xela. How is Félix?"

Suddenly Fernando felt in a hurry to get away. "He's great. I'll let him know I ran into you. Say hello to your dad." He moved on toward the muni, as if remembering his supposed appointment.

When he got home he called Memo to tell him about the stranger looking for his chauffeur. "He's not the only one," Memo told him. "I haven't seen Geraldo in two weeks. The guy has disappeared."

Memo didn't seem concerned about the Mexican. Fernando tried to put his uneasiness out of his mind and attack the pile of student papers on his desk. The university had given him an officemate this year and he preferred to work at home, where he could close the door and be alone. It was a Friday, and he had no classes to teach. The house was quiet, the older children in school and Sandra off somewhere with Omar. He worked steadily through the morning, grading and commenting. At two Tona tapped on the study door to tell him lunch was ready. He took a brief break to eat and went back to work. At four he heard the terrier barking and Sandra's car pulling into the carport. He stretched, glad to be done for the day, and went out to meet her in the courtyard. "Papi, look what Abuelita got me!" Omar held out yet another toy truck, then ran off to add it to his collection.

"How's your mother?" Fernando asked.

"A little better. They've arrested nine suspects in the Salcajá massacre. There are more than a hundred army troops working with the police, so Mamá feels Papá's at less risk. Safety in numbers, I guess. But Papá is still on the case. They think the mastermind is somewhere in Huehuetenango Department."

"That's worrisome." He studied his wife's face, looking for signs that she suspected him of criminal activity. The burden of keeping his secret weighed on him. He felt an unbearable wall between them.

"Now Papá thinks it's the Sinaloa cartel behind it, not the Fuerzas."

"Don Alejandro knows best." He felt slightly reassured. Memo had told him the massacre had nothing to do with their business. "I work for myself. You don't need to know who my associates are," he'd said when Fernando asked him pointblank about the Fuerzas. But Fernando had remained preoccupied. Seeing the Mexican that morning had increased his anxiety. He wished he could open up to Sandra. But that was impossible. If she knew about the lab, knew that he had allowed their son to work there, she would never forgive him.

"Don't forget," she said. "We have to leave for school in an hour."

He had forgotten. Leti's school play was tonight. She and Walter were both going to Francisco Javier now, and Sandra was always on the road. "You must be tired," he said.

"I'll make us some coffee before we go," Sandra said, moving toward the kitchen.

It had started raining by the time they left for Huehue. Fernando turned on the windshield wipers and felt the sound of rain enclose them in a kind of confidentiality, just the two of them alone in the car. "I'm worried," he said. "This massacre. Your father on the hunt for drug dealers." He paused, not knowing how to go on.

"That's his job."

"I'm not sure what Memo is up to out at Sapoclok." It was a crack in the wall. He was desperate to reach her, but didn't know how to do it and preserve her trust in him. He loved his family. He had to convince her of that, that his intentions were good no matter how things had gone awry.

"I know what Memo's doing," she said bitterly. "He's manufacturing crystal meth."

Fernando felt his vision explode into the raindrops on the windshield. For a moment he couldn't see the road. "You know! How? Félix told you."

"Memo told me."

"When?" When had she been talking to Memo?

"When I asked him. I had to know. It's *not* the career I would have chosen for my son." Her voice trembled. "Memo told me about your debt to the loan shark. You got in over your head, he said. It was as if he was trying to excuse you. 'Poor Fernando.'"

He heard harshness in her words. He saw the magnitude of his mistakes through her eyes. How incredible that she knew about the plant, that she'd said nothing to him. He felt himself coming apart. What was going on? How he longed for her forgiveness. "I should have sent Memo away. I should never have agreed to the deal."

"Well, you did." Her voice was curt. He glanced at her, looking for clues to her emotions—anger at him, fear for them. She stared at the windshield wipers, biting her lips. He couldn't look at her for long. The road twisted up from the river and he had to keep his eye on the curves.

"I'm sorry," he said. "Maybe it's not too late. I'm thinking, maybe there's a way to get out of the business. If we could only get Félix away for a few days, send him to visit Emilia in San Cristóbal for a week. We could go to your father. Tell him we have suspicions about what's going on out in the factory, suspicions that Memo is not what we thought. Let your father get the idea to investigate, and…" He paused, struggling for words. "We'd be shocked at what he found." There. He'd said it finally. It didn't sound impossible to him that they could get Memo out of their lives. He could manage, even if he had to go back to the Rattlesnake.

"Darling, we can't do that. Have you thought about what Memo's people would do to us? Remember Salcajá?" Her tone was incredulous. "There's no way out. We have to trust that Memo will protect us."

Trust Memo? What did she know about Memo? "What makes you think…"

He broke off. Coming over the hill facing him was a bus, in his lane, heading directly at them. He honked, adrenaline coursed to his brain, and time slowed down. He saw the bus accelerate toward him, trying to overtake the car it was passing. He began a staccato series of taps on the brakes. He considered the depth of the ditch at his right, and the space between it and the rising embankment, calculating if it could accommodate a large Toyota SUV, deciding it could not. The bus continued to close the distance between them. It was not going to make it out of his lane. He eased toward the ditch. He saw the bus driver's face, contorted with anguish. He felt his tires hit gravel and mud and begin to fishtail. He heard many horns at once, and at a great distance Sandra's scream. He felt the impact of the bus on his left front fender, heard the roar of it passing. He felt the SUV go into a slow rotation and thought about the embankment to his right, the drop-off to his left, as they spun around and changed their orientation toward him. He considered which he would prefer. The road emptied out around him. The scream penetrated his consciousness. The SUV gravitated toward the drop-off. He wondered if that had been his preference. The SUV slid off the road, facing the direction it had come. He hoped that it would be enough, that it would come to a stop. That he would be able to pull it out onto the road again and get them on their way and make it to Francisco Javier in time for Leti's play. But the SUV wasn't finished moving. As it slid over the drop-off he consoled himself that it wasn't deep, just a few meters of grassy slope that ended in brush. The SUV slid sideways and Sandra's side dropped over precipitously. He felt the car roll. He heard crumpling metal and breaking glass. His seatbelt held him in place. Was Sandra's seatbelt fastened? Probably. His hands were still on the steering wheel. He gripped it and waited for the car to stop its tumble. Surely it was slowing down. One more turn and finally, at long last, motion ceased, the SUV resting on its roof in the brush. The blood rushed to his head. Where the windshield had been was the ground, a muddy mess of torn earth, vegetation, and broken glass. He switched off the ignition.

"Sandra. Are you OK?" He could see her strapped to her seat, suspended beside him, her dark hair falling in a mass.

"Oh Fernando! How do we get out of here?" She was crying, but he didn't see blood. Explosion came to his mind. The gas tank could go at any moment. He had to get them out fast. He struggled with his door, got it open. Hanging onto the car seat he took enough pressure off the seatbelt to unbuckle it and crawled out through the open door into the brush. He scrambled to his feet and hacked his way through the bushes around the front of the vehicle. Steam was curling out from the engine well. Rain hissed against the hot undersides. Again he thought of explosion. He clawed his way around to Sandra's door and bent down to see her. She looked out at him through the window. Her tear-streaked face looked wild. "Fernando! Help me! I can't get the door open."

This side of the SUV was badly dented from the roll and the door was caved in. Somehow, the window hadn't broken. Fernando tugged at the handle but it wouldn't budge. He looked around for a tool or a rock. Nothing but bushes and grass. He heard voices from the road above. People ran toward him from the pickup the bus had been passing and from the bus, which had pulled over in front of the pickup. "Bring a tire iron!" he shouted.

Several men crashed down the slope toward him. One brandished a machete. Fernando took the big knife and tried to pry the door open. It still wouldn't yield. "Give me!" the machete's owner said.

Crouching down, he jammed the blade into the slot in the door where the window emerged and jabbed it into the door's interior. "Try the handle now."

The man shimmied the machete blade while Fernando pushed and tugged at the handle. It was past time for the explosion, if there was to be one. Sandra pushed from her side. Fernando knelt by the car so their faces were close through the glass. Hers was upside down, pale, disorienting. Finally a click came from the damaged door, and the button in Fernando's hand gave. He pried the door open, reached inside, put his arms around her, and unfastened her seatbelt. She clung to him while he wrestled her out of the car. When he had her free he lay for a moment in the wet brush with Sandra in his arms. He was breathing heavily from the exertion. Her head was on his chest. He brushed her hair from her face. "Do you have pain anywhere, my love?" he asked.

"I'm all right. How about you?" He felt her shiver.

"You're getting wet," he said. The rain was falling hard.

"Señores, the police are here," the man with the machete said. He helped Sandra to her feet. He took one side of her and Fernando the other and they climbed up the slippery embankment to the road, where a crowd of people stood with umbrellas and shawls over their heads.

The officer from the Remedios police invited him to sit in his patrol car out of the rain while he filed the report. Women from the bus surrounded Sandra and pulled her into the crowd. Fernando watched her go with befuddlement, feeling abandoned. "Good thing you were wearing your seatbelts. Looks like you'll both walk away from this without a scratch," the officer said. "My partner has gone to look for the bus driver and ayudante. People are telling us they ran off. We'll find them. The driver will pay for this. Tell me exactly what happened." He had sheets of forms and a pen in hand.

Fernando was still in the police car, still in shock, when Memo showed up, coming through the crowd with Sandra at his side and tapping on the car window next to Fernando. The policeman rolled down the window. "I'll take Sandra to school and pick up the kids while you wait for the tow truck," Memo said.

Fernando was confused. "How did you get here?" he asked.

Sandra answered with remarkable calm. Perhaps she too was in shock. "I called him. I have to get to school. Leti and Walter are expecting us. They'll be upset." She gave him a penetrating look, as if willing him to believe in the power of her maternal instincts.

Memo! Why hadn't she called Vicente or Elena? Why Memo? He didn't ask. He watched the two of them walk away and get into Memo's car.

11

One month earlier

SANDRA STEPPED OUT OF THE SHOWER, wrapped a towel around herself, and looked through steam at the mirror. It was fogged. She wiped it with a corner of the towel and studied her reflection, looking for the lust angel. Her dark hair was still streaming. She let the beads of water flow down her back. Her cheeks were pink and glistening; her lips were full and quivering with a smile. There he was, the lust angel, breathing in her face, his pink tongue poking through her teeth. She opened the towel and saw his red breath spread across her chest. She felt him spool a wire out from each nipple and give the wires a tug. She held her breath. Her eyes traveled down her torso in the steamy mirror and stroked the hollows between her thighs and pelvis. She felt fingertips, mouthlips brush across her abdomen, trace the stretch marks. She felt oxygen flow to her extremities. Her toes throbbed. Lust angel whispered: *You are beautiful.*

The door behind her in the mirror opened and Memo came in. He was dressed. He smiled at her in the mirror, that smile of his that tightened his thin lips but didn't touch his eyes. "Admiring yourself, Aphrodite?" he asked. He wrapped her wet hair around his fist and gently turned her to face him. "Time for me to go. Are you coming?"

She dropped the towel, leaned into him, felt his body through his clothes. She felt wicked. She licked her tongue across his lips. They responded, grabbed hers; she felt the power of demanding, receiving, sucking, kissing. Then she came to herself, opened her eyes, and pulled back. "I'd better get home before someone notices I'm missing. Just give me a minute to dry my hair."

His hands had found her nipples. He gave them a pinch and stepped away. "Don't be long," he said going out.

Her dryer hung next to the sink in the marble bathroom. She'd helped Memo pick the tiles—a pure and cloudlike white, with the faintest luminous veining. A blameless white. She brushed the column of hot air through her hair, immersed in its roar. Amazing to her that no one had noticed the change in her. That she smiled at things that were not in the room, that she drifted through her days and her duties only half present, listening to a song no one else heard. She went to confession every week and told the priest her little sins. "Bless you, my child," he said. Never, "Is that all? Isn't there something you're leaving out?"

She wasn't stupid. She knew this couldn't last. Sooner or later she'd have to pay. The sky would fall. She'd be discovered. She suffered moments of terror, so she put discovery out of her mind, determined to enjoy her sojourn in the garden of the lust angel while it lasted.

She cut off the dryer and heard doors banging. Memo would be getting impatient. She dressed quickly and went out onto the veranda. Memo was with Geraldo, his new Mexican chauffeur. "I'm taking Doña Sandra home myself. Make yourself useful." His tone was sharp. Disdainful. "You can take the dog for a walk."

Telegram perked up at hearing the word and trotted eagerly toward Memo. "No," he told the dog, "you're going with *Geraldo.*" He signaled, and Telegram sat obediently. Geraldo looked uncomfortable. "Don't rile him and he won't bite," Memo told the Mexican.

"I get the feeling you don't like Geraldo," Sandra said as they drove away.

"You're very perceptive."

No, she thought, she was willfully blind. She hadn't asked him about his past with the Mexicans or about the plant that he and Fernando had built, that Fernando didn't want to talk about. She hadn't asked what Félix was really studying when they sent him away. It was enough then that Félix was rescued. Safe. Now Félix was back, happy and enthusiastic. But her doubts were piling up and her earlier suspicions couldn't remain repressed. "You think your bosses are spying on you."

"My bosses?"

They drove past the plant, lurching over ruts. "You know, rumors have been circulating ever since you arrived that you were involved with drug trafficking. I denied them. I thought you were out of that business. Now my son is working for you. I don't know what he's doing. I'm afraid. Fernando talks about cleaning supplies, but I can tell he's lying. What are you making here?"

"What do you know about a drug called methamphetamine?"

The revelation came from him so easily, so casually, with no fanfare, no avoidance. It was not what she had expected. It was startling. She didn't know what to make of it. "Not much."

"It gives its users an energy boost. In the USA it's very popular. Long-distance truckers take it to stay awake. Students use it to study. Laborers in oil fields, in agriculture, construction, in hard jobs with long hours, use it to help them work.

Single mothers who work two or three jobs need it for energy to take care of their children. It's very valuable."

"Crystal?" Sandra had heard it on TV by this name.

Memo nodded. "That's what Félix learned how to make."

"What! You taught my son to make crystal meth?"

"He's very good at it. He enjoys his work."

He sounded so calm. It could be soap. But no, it was a drug, it was illegal, it was horrifying, it had to be dangerous. The sky was crashing down. Memo was dangerous. She'd known that from the start. "How could you do this! I thought you were helping Félix. Why didn't you tell me the truth?"

"I *was* helping Félix. This is the truth. You don't have to worry. I can guarantee that your son is fine. He doesn't use the drug; he only makes it. There's no risk." They crossed the river and climbed up the opposite hill. Sandra grasped the dashboard to steady herself as the vehicle bounced, her thoughts in turmoil. Memo stopped the car before they reached the first house and killed the engine. He turned to face her. "You can believe me." He reached out and took her hand. "I won't hurt your family."

His touch gave her the usual jolt, but she resisted. "What about your…associates in Mexico? The cartel."

"I have little contact with the cartel. It's all I need and they agree. I operate independently." He pressed her hand to his lips. "Just as you do. It's a thing I admire about you."

Sandra knew when she was being flattered. Romanced. "Don't let this fool you, what we do. My family means everything to me. If anything happens to Félix, or to Fernando…" She broke off, having no idea how she could threaten Memo.

He kissed her fingers and returned her hand to her lap. He looked at her thoughtfully. "I know. My manhood would be in danger." She couldn't help but laugh. He started the car up again and the conversation ended. Had he made her a promise or put her off with a joke? In the year she'd known him, she had watched for signs he was deceiving her, and had found none. He'd treated her with respect, staying away from her when she told him to, welcoming her back when she wanted, answering her questions when she asked. She hadn't asked often. He'd been…honorable.

She debated with herself in the days that followed, but she kept seeing him. She had invited him to her father's birthday party! The invitation had been the impulse of the moment, but part of her wanted to prove some point. That she could survive this double life, that all of them could. Memo had passed the test, charming her parents. Even her sister had said after the visit, "I see why you're all smitten with him. He's very pretty."

"He's Fernando's friend, Carolina," Sandra said into the phone, at once pleased and alarmed at her sister's approval. "Don't get any ideas."

—

Sandra had seen the bus before Fernando did. She saw the lust angel hanging from the bus driver's rear view mirror, and knew that he was coming for her. She would die in sin, her husband at her side, an accusation and a judgment. She had just told Fernando there was no escape. Their names emblazoned across its windshield, the bus came at them. She felt the scream torn out of her by judgment's harsh hand. It reached deep down through her internal organs and pulled up her scream. She deserved her judgment, but she didn't repent. Even when the car was spinning, even when it was tumbling down the embankment, she screamed against her fate.

When she lay in Fernando's arms, cold rain pelting her, feeling tenderness for her husband, his soft embrace, feeling relief that he hadn't paid for her sin, she argued with herself. *I know what I'm doing. It's worth it. How can I go back?*

Scrambling up the embankment, supported by Fernando, she was glad to be alive, free of judgment. While Fernando sat in the police car, she called Memo. She needed to hear his voice. She saw the light of understanding break across Fernando's features when she and Memo left him at the scene of the accident. Even that they would survive. She would fix it. That night, after the accident, Memo had taken her to see the last part of the school play and brought them all home and left before Fernando's return. Fernando came home from his long ordeal with the police and they sat down to a late supper. They didn't talk about Memo. They talked about the accident—the moment Sandra knew the bus was going to hit them—about the play, the children, the damage to the car, whether the bus driver would be captured and forced to pay for its repair.

Only later, when Fernando came to bed, with the light still on, he looked at her with a strange expression and said, "Sandra…what is going on between you and Memo?"

She put her arms around him, buried her face in his neck so as not to stare into his anguish, pulled him close and felt his comforting softness. She felt his heart beating. She couldn't break that heart. "Nothing my love." She wished that could be true. "Don't think about Memo." She felt Fernando's body stiffen in her arms. She wanted him to believe that he was all she needed to be a woman. She wanted to make love to him, but didn't know how. In bed with him she always regressed to feeling like a shy schoolgirl. She reached over him to turn out the light. "Fernando, will you kiss me?" She felt him hesitate, heard him sigh. His arms came to her, his hands moved down her buttocks and thighs to inch up the bottom of her nightgown, and he kissed her.

—

Fernando's SUV went into the shop for repairs. That left Sandra without a car. Walter and Leti took the bus to school. She went to the market every morning on foot, accompanied by Omar, who liked to race up and down the aisles and hide from her. She helped Leti and Walter with their homework. Félix rode his ATV out to the factory every morning, rain or shine.

She walked out to the Pink House on a clear morning, fresh from the night's rain. She took the path through the pinewoods and walked across the riverbed. The gate to Memo's yard was standing open and a police car was parked in front of the veranda. She froze. The plant had been discovered. Their unraveling had begun. She could turn around, leave Memo to his fate. Run to the factory, find Félix, flee. Before she could act, the figures on the veranda turned in her direction. She had another shock. The man with Memo was her father. He saw her.

She walked toward them, foreboding pounding in her chest. Whatever discussion had been going on appeared to have ended abruptly. She spoke quickly. "Papá! What are you doing here?"

"I could ask you that," he said sharply.

"I brought some meals for Memo's freezer." She indicated her shoulder bag. "You don't expect a man to cook for himself?"

"I would expect him to have a cook."

"He's right, Memo. I can ask Tona to look for someone for you."

"Good idea," Memo said, nodding his head once. "But Don Alejandro is here on official business. Apparently a body has been found in the Green Lagoon. How long do you think it's been there?" He turned back to the captain.

"Several weeks. It's badly decomposed. No identification yet."

"Oh dear." Memo sighed. "I may know who it is. My chauffeur disappeared three weeks ago. We'd had a…disagreement. I found him going through my private things. I warned him rather firmly that if it happened again I would let him go. When I discovered that he'd left, taking his personal belongings with him, I assumed that he'd quit his job in a pique and not told me."

"You didn't report him missing?"

"I thought he'd left of his own accord, that he'd decided, as I had, that the relationship wasn't working out."

"What did he take with him?"

"He occupied the shed in back of the house. He had clothes. Nothing else. There was nothing left in his room, so I assumed he carried a suitcase with him."

Sandra listened to this exchange with a peculiar sensation prickling the back of her neck.

"I'll need his name and passport number, and whatever other information you can give me," her father said.

"Of course," Memo said. "I'll get that. Meanwhile, I have some coffee on the stove. Would you like a cup?"

Sandra moved toward the kitchen. "I need to put these things away. Can I get you coffee, Papá?"

"No time. I have to get to the morgue." He fixed her with another piercing stare. She felt his disapproval. She felt like she was ten years old again.

12

June 22

FÉLIX SLUNG HIS PACK DOWN next to Juanito's and found a patch of grass to sit on. Eric stood in front of them, stretched out his arms as if to encompass the world, and exclaimed, "What a view!" He laughed.

They were surrounded by clouds, wispy overhead and in thick banks below. In a few spots they could see through breaks to the valley floor. It had taken them five hours to climb to the top of the volcano. Félix felt tired, but exhilarated. "I warned you," Juanito, their guide, said. "In the dry season—December, January—you can see both coasts from here. Pacific. Caribbean." He pointed in each direction. "But now…"

Kate staggered up the last rise to join them on the bare, windswept summit. She'd had the hardest time with the ascent. Eric threw his arms around her and said something to her in English. She answered and the two Australians sat down next to Juanito and Félix in the shelter of a large boulder that was covered in painted names. It was cold up here, and sweat from the climb began to chill Félix. He put on a fleece. Eric said something more in English to Kate. She switched into her accented Spanish. "At least it isn't raining."

"The descent will take half the time," Juanito said. "We should be back before the rain starts." They'd left Xela before dawn in the van Juanito's company owned, to be on the trail by seven. Félix planned to take the bus back to Huehue that evening, so he could be at work tomorrow. Memo had told him he could take an extra day off if he really needed to, but Félix knew the pressure they were under from the Mexicans to produce more, faster. The demand for product seemed inexhaustible. Félix figured he didn't need an extra day.

His father had told him about running into Juanito in Remedios. His old friend Juanito! It felt like time to get back in touch and Félix called him. Juanito was now off in Xela studying English and tourism and working for Trekker Tours. He'd invited Félix to come (free of charge por supuesto) on this climb up Santa María with the Australian couple. It felt great to get out of the lab and the house and hang out with kids his own age for a change. He was a little jealous of Juanito, who was going to be doing this kind of fun stuff for a living.

They'd eaten their sandwiches on the way up, so Juanito handed around oranges and candy bars while the Australians talked about their travel plans. They had started in Mexico where they learned Spanish and were working their way down, hoping to hit the high points of Latin America—Lake Atitlán and Antigua next, then Copán, Nicaragua (they'd heard good things about Nicaragua), the beaches of Costa Rica, then the itinerary got vague but would definitely include Machu Picchu—in their "gap year." Félix felt his envy of Juanito fade a little. The tour guide would be stuck climbing the same three mountains again and again with people who seemed to be on perpetual vacation.

After they finished their oranges and threw the peels behind the rocks ("Organic waste isn't litter," Juanito said, collecting the candy wrappers), Eric dug into his pack and pulled out a joint. "Anyone care to smoke some marijuana?"

Félix darted an anxious glance at Juanito, whose job it was to handle this. It wasn't that Félix had never smoked pot, but never in such a public place. "Suppose someone shows up," he said.

Eric was cupping his hand around the joint, trying to get it to light. "Don't worry," Juanito said. "No one will care." He sounded as if he spoke from experience. Eric got the joint going and took a long pull.

"The book says Guatemala is super tough on drugs," Kate said. She took the joint Eric passed her.

"Only for the little fish," Juanito said. "The real narcos do what they want, go where they want."

Eric leaned back on the rock, tipped his head back and let out the smoke. "So would you say that Guatemala is a narco state?"

Félix bridled inside. The way Eric said it sounded like a slur. Félix would bet there were drugs and corruption in Australia too. Juanito just shrugged and said, "Could be." He took his turn on the joint, then passed it to Félix. He filled his lungs and held the smoke in. "I'll tell you a story," Juanito said. "Happened to me up in San Marcos. I was driving the support vehicle to meet a group of bicyclists who were crossing the mountains. I got a flat tire and didn't have a jack. I was in the middle of nowhere, no cell signal, no one on the road, and I didn't know what to do. Along comes a convoy, five or six big expensive SUVs—Land Cruisers, Escalades, that kind of thing—and they all pull over. Guys with machine guns jump out and surround me."

"Were you scared?" Kate leaned forward, straining to follow the Spanish.

"You bet! I figured my number was up." He took the joint as it came around again. The marijuana was strong, and Félix was starting to feel its effects.

Juanito went on. "A big guy with a round face asked me what I was doing there. I explained I was working for tourists. So they all got back in their SUVs and went on except for a few guys in a pickup truck who stayed behind and helped me change my tire."

"Did you find out who they were?" Eric asked.

"I didn't want to know. I didn't want to know what they had in their vehicles."

Félix thought about the trucks that moved chemicals and products in and out of Eco-Clean. They seemed a lot more discreet than a convoy of flashy cars. Who was operating that convoy? What were they carrying?

"In San Marcos they love their drug lord. He gives them jobs, builds them schools, keeps the peace."

"The peace?" Kate asked skeptically.

"Violence is bad for business. The Chamale doesn't allow it."

"The what?" Kate asked.

"It's his name, their own local narco kingpin. Much preferable to the Mexicans, who give drug trafficking a bad name." How did Juanito know all this? A lot more than Félix knew. Félix remained quiet, listening uncomfortably.

Juanito went on, an easy talker. "Another time I was kayaking with five tourists—just three kayaks—on Lake Izabal." Félix had no idea Juanito got around so much. "A storm came up in the wide part of the lake, the Golfete, and we had to take shelter up a creek. We came upon a big mansion, very luxurious, and the caretaker invited us to come inside and dry out. Inside I saw piles of dollars that had been spread out to dry so they wouldn't mildew. The caretaker was very nice to us, gave us hot coffee, told us the owner wasn't there right now."

"So, were they laundering the money do you suppose?" Eric asked.

Juanito grinned. "I guess so!"

"In Australia, the drug lord's biggest problem is how to launder all that money," Kate said.

So he'd been right, Félix thought. Australia had its drug traffickers, too. He thought about the mansion on Izabal. He hadn't seen any stacks of money coming into the Pink House. Memo must have something worked out, but he hadn't told Félix, who just earned a salary. A good salary, what a bank clerk would make. "I don't think that would be such a problem in Guatemala," he said. It was his first contribution to the discussion. "Portillo got away with laundering seventy million dollars while he was president." The ex-president had been in the news lately; acquitted by Guatemalan courts, he was being extradited to the US for using a Miami bank for his cleansing operation.

Juanito laughed. "The president who stole from school children. Nice guy. And he was rich to begin with. He needed more?"

"The rich always need more," Félix said. "Not like us." Deliberate irony. He thought about his father borrowing money from the Rattlesnake, another secret Félix was wise to, his father going in on a meth lab, scrounging to find money to fix his car after it gets wrecked and the slimebucket bus driver disappears. His poor dad, always coming up short, always needing more.

By this time the joint was finished. They all watched the clouds billow and form below them. "Look," Juanito said pointing. "That's smoke from Santiaguito." The active side cone off Santa María was visible below them. "It last erupted in 2003."

"You guys live in a dangerous country," Eric said. "If the volcanoes and earthquakes don't get you, the narcos will."

"In my experience," Juanito said, "the narcos are nice to you if you don't get involved in their disputes."

"So what are you saying?" Eric asked. "You're OK with being a narco state?"

"Eric!" Kate said. "That's not fair. Juanito doesn't run Guatemala."

"If I ran Guatemala, it would all be legal!" Juanito said. "Cocaine, heroin, crystal." Félix kept his face from betraying his shock. It was the first he'd heard meth mentioned. But he shouldn't be surprised that Juanito knew of its existence, considering how informed he was. "Let them be controlled and taxed like alcohol. The war on drugs kills more people than the drugs do. Or volcanoes."

"I'm all for legalizing marijuana," Kate said. "But I draw the line at meth. It's wicked stuff, horrible what it does to people." Félix remained silent.

"Is everybody rested?" Juanito asked. "We'd better get going."

On the way down a gentle rain started, turning the steep trail to slippery mud. They put on their rain shells but their spirits were undampened. Eric and Kate tried to slide down the trail as if they were on skis, laughing uproariously when they landed on their butts. When they'd descended the mountain and dropped the Australians off at their hostel in Xela to shower and dry off, Juanito called his boss. "Good news!" he told Félix. "I can run you home. I'm picking up some tourists in Huehue in the morning and the jefe says I can have the van for the night."

It had been a long day. Félix was glad of the ride, and of Juanito's companionship. He felt at ease with him and relaxed from all the strenuous exercise. Juanito's attitude toward drugs was on his mind as they drove past the turnoff to Salcajá. He pointed to the sign. "You heard about the massacre?" he asked. Of course Juanito had heard, it was all over the news. "My grandfather's working on the case. My grandmother's crazy with worry."

"I don't blame her," Juanito said. "Those police in Salcajá double-crossed the wrong cartel. You don't want to mess with the Fuerzas."

"He doesn't think it was the Fuerzas. He thinks it was some bunch from the Huistas." San Antonio Huista and Santa Ana Huista were little towns in the northwestern part of the department of Huehuetenango.

"Well, I wouldn't want to be a cop these days, corrupt or straight."

"When would you have ever wanted to be a cop?" Félix asked.

"Good point! All I ever wanted to do is climb mountains and ride my bicycle. Hey, are you still riding?" Juanito had introduced Félix to mountain biking in his first year of high school. Félix had been thrilled to find a sport that he enjoyed, that didn't involve teams and competition. They'd trained together until they could bicycle all the way up to the altiplano, a climb of four thousand feet.

"No. After you graduated I got involved in…other things." Like falling in love and getting his heart broken, but he didn't want to talk about that.

"Man, you have to get out more. You can't spend all your time working in that lab. It's unhealthy, even if you are making environmentally friendly stuff." Félix hadn't told Juanito much about his job and was worried he might start asking more specific questions. "You look pale and you've kind of thinned out. We need to bulk you up. Let's go biking next weekend if I don't have to work."

The van's engine struggled and Juanito shifted down. They'd passed Cuatro Caminos and the highway climbed toward Huehue, twisting through mountains. "Yeah, you're right. I have been pretty cooped up in the lab. There's a lot of pressure, getting a new business off the ground." Without meaning to he sighed.

Juanito glanced over at him. "A lot of worries?" Juanito was perceptive. Maybe he *had* heard about Félix's troubles with Gloria. Or maybe he had heard other things. "Don't worry about your grandfather," Juanito said. "He's a legend in Huehuetenango. He's tough."

13

June 28

FERNANDO NEEDED TO BE ALONE. He paced the courtyard patio and felt his house closing in on him, felt la Tona's eyes on him. He couldn't go back into his home office. It was impossible to sit still and focus on his students' papers. One more pass around the geraniums, doves cooing with annoying insistence, and he left the house, shutting the door quietly behind him. Down the street he walked quickly past his sister's house, not wanting her to look out of her tiny shop and see him go by. He didn't turn toward the park, where he would be sure to run into acquaintances. His guts were roiling, as they had been ever since the accident. He was exhausted. He hadn't been getting enough sleep. He would lie awake in bed at night listening to Sandra snoring next to him. They hadn't talked about Memo. He'd tried, the night of the accident. But they'd ended up making love. The next day she'd acted as if their lives had gone back to normal. She was busy, efficient, calm—and distant.

He found himself on the outskirts of town at the gate to the cemetery. Well, that was a good place to be alone, and even if he ran into the caretaker, he would assume that Don Fernando was there to commune with the dead and leave him be. He went in and turned down the first aisle to walk between the rows of tombs. The houses of the dead rose on either side of him like small apartment buildings, each belonging to a family of Remediosinos. Their plain cement façades were painted in pastel pinks and blues and golds, their stacked niches overflowing with flowers, a miniature city, tidy and orderly, like Remedios. The names engraved on each niche in the family mausoleums were familiar to him—his townspeople, his neighbors, his relatives, his own parents. There were unfilled niches in the Granados family tomb waiting for his brothers, himself, Sandra.

Sandra. When she and Memo had walked away into the rain—no, Memo's arm was not around her, but it might as well have been—he hadn't been able to breathe. He'd turned back to the policeman sitting next to him in the car who was asking him questions and the words suddenly sounded like gibberish. He'd thought his head would explode with disbelief and rage. But he'd taken a few deep gulps of air and forced himself to focus on the policeman, on answering questions and filling out forms. His anger simmered until that night when Sandra turned to him and asked for love, and even through the familiar act it was hard to tell love from rage. At the end his rage crawled back into the empty cave of his heart, and he fell asleep, exhausted.

Since then he'd been unable to confront her, unable to force her to tell him a truth he didn't want to hear. They'd been like inmates on death row since the accident; he knew that one more wrong move would mean the end of their marriage. He couldn't bear that.

He reached the end of the avenue of tombs and turned past the caretaker, who was pushing a wheelbarrow full of gardening tools. The city of the dead was mostly cement, aisles and tombs, but occasional flowerbeds had been carved into the concrete. Beyond the cemetery walls the silent mountains rose to the altiplano. It was an ideal spot for pacing. Fernando turned down the next aisle of tombs.

In all their years together—nineteen years—he'd never doubted Sandra's fidelity, never imagined her leaving him. It was inconceivable. Even now, with the evidence before his eyes, it was hard to comprehend. Other men's wives cheated, not his. Sandra was too honorable, too religious, too...perfect. He'd always relied on her. He couldn't live without her. (Hadn't he heard those words, coming from his son not so long ago, and hadn't he said that life goes on, or some such bromide? But adolescent heartbreak was not to be compared with...nineteen years!) He thought back over those years, pictured her at her desk in the classroom where he first saw her. How elegant and reserved she had been. She was such a serious student, not like these airheads of today. He'd found her irresistible from the start. Hadn't he tried to resist? After all, relations between professor and student were frowned upon. And she had been ambitious about her education. In the end, though, love had triumphed. She'd quit university, they'd married, and he had brought her out of her shell; she'd grown in grace and confidence over the years, more beautiful with each child.

He reached the end of the aisle and turned again to the next row of tombs. The tombs went on, row upon row. All the lives lived here, now over, all troubles extinguished, hopes buried in cement. Fernando had never thought much about the afterlife, but it had comforted him to know he would spend it here, surrounded by his people, Sandra at his side. Without her, all permanence was gone, his sense of order was upended.

And the townspeople: what about them—did they know? He felt the hot breath of shame. The word *cuckold* came to him. Humiliation. How could she do this to him? His anger burned. The sun was hot in the cemetery and he was working up a sweat. How could he have let this go on?

Cuckolded by Memo. His thoughts shifted away from Sandra, where thinking was too painful. Memo! Was this his revenge? Had he been planning this from the first day Fernando had taken him home to lunch? He'd had his eye on Sandra that day, Fernando was sure. That's when he'd begun his seduction. Of course! He must have been laughing at Fernando this whole time, the absent-minded college professor too blind to see what was going on before his eyes. He had to have it out with Memo. But how?

He visualized confronting Memo. Angry words, shouting rising to a crescendo, his fist smashing into Memo's hard stomach, into his face. He tried to imagine blood spurting from Memo's nose or the crunch of a breaking jaw. But all he could see were his blows bouncing off his enemy's iron body, Memo's lips curling in a sneer. What did a man do, a peaceful man like himself, up against a trained assassin?

He knew what men did, from the daily news reports, from the telenovelas, from firsthand accounts of neighbors and acquaintances and witnesses. A man could betray his rival to his enemy. But giving away Memo would mean betraying himself, and his son. Some men hired killers to do their dirty work. Fernando figured he could find a hired killer, some peasant desperate enough to do anything for 500 quetzales. Was that enough? He had no idea. The Rattlesnake would know. The Rattlesnake! No, he couldn't go that route and get himself back into debt to that scum. He could imagine the

Rattlesnake's hired thug failing and Memo standing over his bleeding corpse and laughing at the hit man's incompetence and Fernando's cowardice. He saw Memo put his arm around Sandra's waist and walk away with her, remarking, *What a wimp you married!*

His imagination spinning to the point of madness, he reeled his thoughts in. A real man had to face his rival, but he had to even the odds. He had to strike when it was unexpected. He had to use his wits. Fernando continued his relentless back and forth among the aisles of the dead, weighing risks, testing probabilities, until he was done with thinking, ready to test the theories with action. On his way out of the cemetery he passed the caretaker, whose wheelbarrow was now full of weeds.

When he got home the car was in the driveway and Sandra at the patio table helping Leti and Walter with their homework. She greeted him with her usual serenity and he steeled himself against cozy domesticity. "I need the car keys," he said. "I have a meeting at the university."

No sense telling her where he was really going, and giving her a chance to warn Memo. She handed him the keys without complaint.

"I might be late," he said, casting a furtive longing look at his kids, as if it might be his last.

"Drive carefully," she said.

Before leaving he went up to his bedroom and selected a loose-fitting windbreaker that wouldn't show a bulge in its pocket. He kept an old pistol in a locked drawer beside the bed. Nothing fancy, but adequate protection against intruders. He kept it loaded, with a box of bullets next to it. He slipped both items into his pockets, took one last look around as if he might be forgetting something, and left.

On his drive out to Sapoclok Fernando let his sense of shame take control and nurse the flames of hatred. He had never shot at a human target; his studies had kept him out of the army during the war. But this would be to his advantage. Memo wouldn't expect him to resort to violence. Memo would feel secure in his reputation as a killer, thinking Fernando didn't have the balls to protect his own. Thinking he could manipulate the gullible professor, taking over his property and seducing his wife and that Fernando would remain forever weak and ignorant. That he hadn't confronted Sandra was also to his advantage. Memo wouldn't suspect that Fernando knew the truth. Fernando had to keep hold of his advantage and catch Memo unaware. He drove past the plant toward the house, hoping to find Memo there. He got to the gate. The black Land Cruiser was parked in the carport. That was good. The gate was locked. There was nothing to do but pull out his phone and act casual, the impulsive, ebullient old Fernando that Memo knew.

"Hey, Memo. I'm right outside. Just decided on the spur of the moment to drop by."

The door to the Pink House opened, and Memo walked down the veranda as the automatic gate opened. Fernando pulled inside, parked behind the Land Cruiser and got out. "I hope I'm not catching you at a bad time."

"Not at all," Memo said giving him a welcoming slap on the shoulder. "An unexpected pleasure. Come on in. Have a beer?"

"Why not?" Fernando said and followed Memo down the veranda toward the kitchen, slipping a hand into his jacket pocket. There was no sign of anyone else around, not even the Doberman. Fernando's heart was racing.

When Memo was opening the refrigerator door, his back to Fernando, that would have been the time to do it, but

Fernando was not one who could shoot a man in the back with no warning. Instead, he pressed the barrel of the pistol against Memo's back and said, "No sudden movements. Place your hands against the refrigerator."

"Fernando! You're kidding!"

Fernando gave the gun a poke. "No," he said. "Spread your legs apart." Memo complied, and Fernando patted him down, feeling an awkward loathing at touching his enemy's body. He found no weapons. "Let's go sit down. Keep your hands in the air." With his gun trained on Memo, Fernando followed him into the dining room. "Hands on the table," he barked when Memo sat. Fernando had great respect for those hands, which reputedly had been trained as weapons. He remained standing, looking down on his adversary. Standing gave him the feeling he was maintaining his advantage, but could he shoot a man who was sitting in a chair? He pressed on. "How long have you been sleeping with my wife?"

Memo's forehead wrinkled in concern. His eyes shone directly into Fernando's. "Nando, Nando," he sighed. "You're angry. I understand. I know what you're feeling. I assure you: Sandra loves you. She would never leave you. But there are times when a woman has to, how shall I say it? Break out. She had never been with any man but you. You know that! This was something she had to get out of her system."

"What." Fernando's hand on the gun trembled. He wrapped his other hand around the wrist to steady it. "*What* was something she had to get out of her system?"

"An adventure. She's a bold woman. That's why you love her. I admire you both, care for you both. I assure you, this little adventure meant nothing to her."

"Are you saying it's over?"

"Of course it's over. Sit down. Let's talk. I don't like to see you so upset."

"Was it over last week when she called you from the accident?" Fernando didn't sit. He kept the gun pointed at Memo, but with less conviction. Whether he could believe Memo or not, what did it matter? The "adventure" had happened; it was a fact, unavoidable, unforgivable.

"That was a mistake. She had been careful to be discreet, careful not to hurt you. But the accident…you were both shaken up. It was important to get to the school. She knew she could rely upon me, that was all. You both can rely on me. She didn't stop to think about how…you would take it."

How was a man to take his wife's betrayal? There was only one way. "This is bullshit, Memo! I should just shoot you now and get it over with."

"And I would understand if that was your decision. You could kill me with impunity so far as the local authorities go, I have no doubt. At their best the Huehue police are pretty ineffectual. And your father-in-law would be a help. He was out here today, by the way."

"Don Alejandro? What was he doing here?" Fernando's arm was getting tired. He sat down across from Memo and rested his elbow on the table, the gun still aimed at him.

"They found a body in the Green Lagoon. Remember my chauffeur who disappeared? What do you know! I thought he'd gone back to Mexico."

"How did he get into the Green Lagoon?"

"If it is even him. No one knows. I promised Don Alejandro I would cooperate with the investigation." Memo paused and looked down at his hands spread out on the table. Fernando felt sick. "Nando, you have to think about your family.

If anything were to happen to me, the cartel would not leave you alone. You and I go way back. We can work out our differences." Fernando felt his anger curl up into a furry ball in the pit of his stomach. Memo looked him in the eyes again. "You don't want to work with the Mexicans. Believe me."

14

July 17

MEMO STOPPED AT THE GUARD BOOTH and rolled down his window. "The general is expecting me," he said, handing his identification to the corporal on duty. The corporal flipped through pages in a binder. Memo waited patiently. He was used to this. This corporal was new to guard duty, but new or old, the routine didn't vary, always the tedious military bureaucracy. The corporal shook his head. "Your clearance isn't here."

"Look again," Memo said.

The corporal plodded through the binder a second time, studying each page slowly as if it were an ancient text in a yet untranslated hieroglyphic, comparing it to Memo's ID as a possible Rosetta stone. Finally he said, "Here it is." Painstakingly he copied information from the ID into the binder. He handed the ID and a pass to Memo. "You know the way?"

"I know the way." He pulled past the guard and drove into the Military Zone. The vivid memory of his arrival at this place thirty years earlier would never fade, although he'd forgotten much of his military service, deliberately erased it from his mind. The night of his abduction from the safe house—henceforth to be called his recruitment—he'd been seventeen, shivering with cold and fear. He and the other recruits were dumped from the back of the military truck. The dark-faced sergeant who had stuck his Galil in Memo's face stripped off his clothes. "Say goodbye to your fancy pants," he'd chortled, then forced him to sit naked on a bench while his head was shaved. Rough hands had shoved him into a cold shower and scrubbed him with lye; then the sergeant had thrust at him an olive green uniform, coarser and more worn than the school uniform he'd taken away. "Let's go!" he'd barked to the six recruits.

Still damp and chattering from cold, Memo had followed the other recruits into a large dim barrack. Snores came from rows of bunks. At one end of the barrack the cement floor was lined with straw pallets. "We're short on beds," the sergeant had said, handing him a thin blanket. "Sweet dreams!"

Exhausted, Memo had dropped into a deep sleep and dreamed of drowning in ice water. Every time he came sputtering to the surface, the butt of a Galil whacked him down under again. This had repeated over and over until a loud bell and shouts woke him. Feeling like he'd hardly slept, he'd followed the other recruits outside for an hour of running around a dirt track. Shouted abuses kept him going, past the point he thought his heart would explode. Through a chain link fence he glimpsed green playing fields, basketball courts, and streets of well-kept houses, beckoning like an oasis. He thought it must be some colonia in a part of Huehue he didn't know. When they were finally allowed to stop running and stand at attention, gasping for breath, he'd asked the recruit beside him what was on the other side of the fence. The boy had given him a strange look. The drill sergeant had overheard the question and grabbed Memo's nose, giving it a painful twist. "You're looking at the officers' quarters, scumbag," he'd said with a smirk. "Welcome to the largest base in Central America, population 20,000 soldiers. I repeat, *soldiers*. Real men."

Around the outer perimeter of the base the chain link was festooned with ranks of coiled razor wire, the top row of which was electrified. In the days of basic training that followed, grueling days of hard sweat under the sun and humiliation at the hands of drill sergeants, Memo gazed at the officers' quarters. The ordered streets and green fields mocked him. There was no escape to civilian life. All that waited for him there was a mud-floored hut and the shame of poverty. With every day of pounding around the track, his dream of success—through university study, aided by his ties with the wealthy Carillo family—died another death. Anita Carillo and college wouldn't be waiting for him when the war was over, his pounding feet told him. The war had been going on forever, since long before he was born; it would never end, his aching lungs told him. Every day of basic he ran around the track and through courses, his body loaded with heavy equipment and armament. His body, already fast, hardened. The vision of the officers' quarters gradually morphed from mockery to lure. He wouldn't give up. He had been the soccer star of Francisco Javier; he could make it into the elite of the military—the special forces. The Kaibiles became his new ambition. Rather than balk under the sergeants' threats and blows, he turned all his energy toward rising to the top of his class of recruits, preparing himself for the onerous entrance tests into Kaibil training.

Thirty years later the razor wire that had surrounded the Military Zone was gone, giving it an open, almost park-like appearance, albeit an overgrown weedy park. Since the Peace Accords in '96, the base had shrunk. Most of the barracks had been shuttered, cracks and mudholes had appeared in many of the courts and playing fields, and the officers' housing had a look of abandonment. Scarcely three thousand soldiers remained, under the command of his old friend Lieutenant General Arcadio Baldomero Arellano y Torre. Memo wound through the sad streets, parked in an unnumbered space, and crossed the broken pavement toward the dilapidated headquarters, carrying his briefcase. The sergeant at the front gate recognized him but still made a show of looking at his pass and ID. "Tell the general I'm here, if you don't mind," Memo said.

After the usual wait while messages made their way through the crackling phone system, a second sergeant appeared at the gate. "The general can see you." Memo allowed himself to be patted down. "I have to look inside your briefcase."

"Of course," Memo said with the flicker of a smile.

The sergeant looked and grunted. "Follow me," was all he said.

Memo followed down a corridor of peeling linoleum, through another gate, past a guard to the door of the general's office. The sergeant knocked. "Come in." The sergeant opened the door and Memo went in. "That will be all," the general said, and the sergeant left, closing the door behind him.

"Memo! How goes the detergent business? Everything peaceful out at Sapoclok?" Arellano stood up behind his cluttered desk, shook Memo's hand and waved him into a chair.

"Not bad. I brought you a little something that just came in." Memo drew out a bottle of Laphroaig single malt. "1974," he added.

"I don't know about Scotches, but that was a good year for me. I got my first horse, a gift from my grandfather. We'd better taste it." He opened a drawer in his desk and took out two glasses. "Will you do the honors?"

Memo uncorked the Scotch and poured just one finger in his glass, two in the general's. They took a moment to inhale the fumes and sip the drink, then Memo said, "Any news on the Salcajá investigation?"

"Oh well, you know, we've rounded up a few minor players up in the Huistas. The so-called ringleader will be tracked down sooner or later. These idiots have to be thrown to the wolves, you realize. They screwed up. Shooting up a police station, how stupid does it get?" The general snorted, then added in a dry tone, "We can't have narcos operating with impunity in Guatemala. Your friends understand this, I hope."

"They do. You don't have to worry," Memo said. "There is something you can help me with. Our local police captain is getting too interested in a body that turned up on the Granados property. This would be a good time to transfer him up to Nenton to chase after narcos up there."

"Should be no problem. What was this body doing out your way?"

"Going for a swim in a secluded little pond. Seems he got a cramp. Somehow he must have got caught in a snag, since it took several weeks for the body to surface. They think he was a Mexican national."

"Anyone your friends know?" the general asked.

"Well, yes. But I don't think they'll be weeping bitter tears. They have other things on their minds."

"F-40's arrest. That's shaking things up. I'm concerned. Some say the organization is breaking down," Arellano said.

"F-40 was a fucking loose canon and an asshole. Without F-3 at the top there's no discipline. I don't like it. I'm a military man."

"You have to be careful."

"I always am. My business is independent, and, as you know, it's doing well." Memo stood up. "You're a busy man. I don't want to impose on your time."

The general put his arm around Memo's shoulders and walked him to the door of his office. "Good to see you, brother. You can count on me to watch your back."

"For sure, Arcadio. I always could," Memo said. A waiting sergeant escorted Memo back toward the front gate.

If it hadn't been for Arcadio Baldomero, Memo might not have made it through El Infierno, the Kaibil training camp. In their first week of training Arcadio had been assigned Memo's "brother" to eat, sleep, and work together all the time. If one made a mistake, both were punished. The jungle heat, the incessant biting of a billion insects, the taste of fetid river water, the iron taste of his own blood when he sucked his self-inflicted wound under orders, the extreme physical training coupled with sleep deprivation combined to break as many recruits as possible. One night, a month into the training, Memo and Arcadio had slipped silently through the forest on patrol. Gunfire had crackled from every direction. Their own or the enemy's? Their commanders kept them in suspense to increase the psychological pressure. "Freeze!" Memo remembered Arcadio's hoarse whisper. They had listened to the guns and smelled the stink of fear in each other's sweat. Not the familiar coughing noise of the Galil, but the sluggish crack of an AK 47. Guerrillas, close by. Here in the Kaibil stronghold. Here in hell.

"Down," Arcadio had murmured. They had slithered to the ground and Memo followed Arcadio, crawling through black muck, scraping over tree roots, getting tangled in vines, away from the gunfire. Interesting, Memo remembered thinking at the time, how being under fire puts all other fears—of poisonous snakes and spiders, of future punishment for deserting your post—into perspective. They had come to a mud bank. Starlight had showed dimly on the surface of a sluggish river. Dark forms of other soldiers splashed neck-deep in the water. Easy for the guerrillas to pick off, Memo had thought. The camp was on the other side. Together they had entered the water, keeping low. The muddy bottom sucked at their boots. They had waded in deeper and deeper. Their uniforms, backpacks, rifles weighed them down. Memo had thought that night he might die, dragged down by his equipment to drown, hit by a guerrilla's bullet, torn apart by a crocodile. He was so exhausted by the many long days and nights of training, he no longer felt he could resist death. He was ready to sink down and let it take him, relieve him from the stress of trying to stay alive. He stumbled and felt Arcadio grab him in the armpit. "Come on, man," Arcadio hissed. "We're almost there."

Later, when they found out that there had been no guerrillas, that the ambush was staged, that one trainee had died, hit by a "guerrilla" bullet, Arcadio had laughed out loud and shaken his head. "Those sons-of-bitches," he said. "They had us shitting in our pants."

He and Arcadio had been among the seven who graduated to wear the maroon beret, seven survivors of the sixty who had entered the training that year. The bonds they'd formed in El Infierno had survived thirty years, through the twists of their subsequent fates. Of course, it didn't hurt that in addition to the loyalty they'd forged as comrades in arms, Memo was making regular deposits into the general's offshore account. Arcadio's cut in the business was generous, but Memo didn't begrudge it.

Outside the general's headquarters, Memo hurried to his car. His next pressing task was lunch with Fernando. Since Fernando's attempt to kill him, it was more important than ever to salvage his old friend's pride. Poor Fernando! He was so unsuited to violence. Memo had known the moment he'd felt the pistol's barrel at his back that it would not go off. Still, the confrontation had been inevitable; Sandra had been bound sooner or later to let their affair out. Now it would require all his resources to convince Fernando that actually, none of this mattered. Their lives could go on as before, even if their relationships were complicated. Fernando and Sandra, what an irony! He was not a sentimental man and yet, he loved them both. Not that he would ever tell either one.

He drove into Huehue from the Military Zone, mulling over the career that had landed him back where he'd begun, like some sort of homing pigeon. Arcadio had risen in rank. No surprise there; the military was still class conscious. Was it to further degrade them that their trainers at El Infierno had paired well-born Arcadio with a poor half-Indian? Once out of hell, the Arellano y Torre name had opened doors into the cofradía, that secretive club of higher commanders that engineered the brutal tactics the army had used to win the war. Arcadio had never actually told him about the cofradía, although they'd stayed in touch. He didn't have to. From his years in the jungle Memo had senses that went beyond other men's. He figured things out. With peace, and the reduction in the size of the army, it was only natural that the cofradía would shift its activities.

Arcadio had hinted at some of this when they'd met up again in the Petén in '99. The adrenaline and horror of combat behind him, Memo was back at El Infierno as an instructor, dissatisfied with his own rank and getting bored with putting recruits through their paces now that the war was over. Arcadio had come up from the capital, looked him up and invited him for a drive off the base. They'd ended up in a walled compound in the jungle, in the living room of a sprawling mansion that seemed empty except for servants, sipping single malt. When Memo asked whose house it was, Arcadio was vague. "A military friend, you don't need to know him, who's exploring business opportunities in Mexico with me."

"Mexico?"

"Exporting advanced paramilitary training to organizations that can pay a little better than the Guatemalan army. We have a valuable brand: Kaibil."

"*'If I advance, follow me. If I stop, urge me on. If I retreat, kill me.'*"

Arcadio chuckled. "You know where the Kaibil motto comes from?"

"I believe it was a French royalist general who failed to stem the Revolution," Memo said. "He could have used some Kaibiles."

"Touché. So, are you interested in Mexico? We could use your talents."

Memo had gone to Mexico. He was back in the environment that kept him alive, where every sense was attuned, every move counted, and he was finally making some money.

His thoughts broke off abruptly when he reached the entrance to Casa Real and pulled into its courtyard. It had been more than two weeks since he and Fernando had had lunch together. He'd given Fernando a cooling off period, then called him this morning to suggest they resume their weekly ritual. Fernando's voice on the phone had sounded wooden. "I'll be there," he said, but clearly he was not looking forward to it. Memo was determined to win back Fernando's trust. By the time Fernando entered the restaurant, Memo was sitting at their usual table by the fireplace with a bottle of wine opened and ready.

"Let's drink to old times," he said, filling Fernando's glass.

"Whatever you say, Memo." Fernando avoided his eyes.

"Did I ever tell you about my wife?" he began.

Fernando looked taken aback. "I didn't know you had a wife."

"I did. In Mexico." Memo sighed heavily. "I met her in a club in Mexico City, the DF. She was a model." He watched Fernando raise his eyes to him with a glimmer of interest. He continued, wrapping the story around Fernando and drawing him in. "She'd grown up poor, like I did, then won a beauty contest when she was sixteen. She parlayed that win into a career in the cutthroat modeling business. Not just a pretty face, she was smart without book learning, and she had a strong character. Oh boy, did she! You couldn't push her around. We fell in love." He smiled sheepishly.

Fernando's eyes were still on him. "Why are you telling me this?" he asked.

Memo could hear the rage and humiliation still seething in Fernando's voice. He spread his hands, palms up, empty of guile. "I want you to know more about me. It's painful to talk about this, but you deserve it. Carmen gave up her career to marry me and move to Matamoros. I worked on a ranch outside of the city. I told her I was the manager of a huge hacienda."

"She believed you?" Fernando cut in.

"For a while. She was a good Catholic. I didn't want her to know the truth."

"Which was?"

"The ranch was a training camp for an elite force of bodyguards. You know them as the Fuerzas." Memo used the word *them,* and not *us.*

"So, your marriage was built on a lie." Fernando's voice was harsh.

Memo gave him a rueful smile. "You could say that," he said and drained his wineglass. The waiter arrived, put their steaks in front of them, and refilled their glasses. "Bon appétit!" Memo said.

Fernando looked at his steak without appetite, but picked up his fork.

"I'd say our marriage was built on love," Memo said. "We lived in a big house in Matamoros. Carmen raised our three children—two girls, a little boy. It was a good life...until Carmen found out." He broke off, as if at a loss for words.

"Found out what?" Fernando goaded. "That you were a criminal? A killer of men?"

"I was an instructor. I trained the Fuerzas in the same techniques I learned in the army. I taught discipline. But Carmen saw it as you do; she threatened to leave and take the children with her, never let me see them again." He poured the last of the wine into Fernando's glass and signaled to the waiter to bring another bottle.

"I begged her to stay. I'm not the tough guy you think I am. I promised her I would never kill again. She stayed. But she kept me on a short leash: church every Sunday, money to good causes." Memo closed his eyes and raised a thumb and forefinger to squeeze the tiredness from them as the waiter poured more wine. "I was a regular Boy Scout."

"A Boy Scout working for gangsters. Very nice."

Memo nodded. "It's not an easy outfit to leave. Loyalty is strictly enforced." He washed his last bite of steak down with wine. "I should have, though. I should have picked up my family and run. But I didn't have the balls." He stopped.

"What happened?" Fernando was caught up in the story. Either that, or he relished Memo's admission of weakness.

"The Gulf Cartel killed them. A dispute between the Gulf and the Fuerzas. I came home one day and found seven bodies lined up in my patio: my wife, my three children—my youngest, my boy, was just two—the hired girl, the gardener, and the dog. They were carefully arranged by the killers. We never found out how the killers got in; the neighbors heard nothing, or so they said. All the bodies, except for the dog, were missing their heads."

"My God!"

"The heads were delivered to my boss."

Fernando looked sick. "How can you work with these people?"

"I couldn't. I left Matamoros. For a while I stayed in Veracruz. The organization tried to compensate me for my loss. Hah! I told them I needed to go home, and start over." He put emphasis on the word *home*.

"So here you are," Fernando said. "Still in the business."

"A man has to live," Memo said with another sigh. "You have to live too, Fernando."

"Right." He sounded bleak. Memo sensed the rage draining out of Fernando. The man wasn't built for holding onto revenge. Resignation was creeping in.

"I never thought I'd have feelings again, Fernando. I've found family again, here, with you…and Sandra."

Fernando startled. "You have a hell of a definition of family."

"Perhaps. But I'm sincere. I have to ask. How are things between you and Sandra?"

"Fuck you, Memo."

"Look," Memo said, "I've been told, but I wouldn't know, that a little sojourn—how can I put this?—off the straight and narrow can act as an aphrodisiac in a long marriage. I wondered if that was the case for you." Especially since he'd called Sandra and told her that her marriage was at risk and she might want to be nice to her husband. She'd been stunned when he told her what her husband had threatened. As if she hadn't thought him capable of such rage. As if she hadn't realized how badly she could hurt him. Memo had heard the remorse in her voice. Knowing Sandra, her penitence wouldn't last. Memo didn't think their affair was over, despite what he'd told Fernando, just that it had entered a new and more delicate phase.

"Well, maybe so. She's been more open. Not that we've talked about you."

"I wouldn't do that. Women just get defensive."

Fernando looked at him with an expression that told him *Don't be such a fucking expert.* "But we're talking more like we used to. And she's been…affectionate." Fernando looked past him with tight lips.

"Sexy?"

"You know I don't talk about my wife that way!" Fernando exploded.

"And that's the problem. You make her feel too pure, Fernando. You need to make her feel dirty sometimes. Just imagine that she's Anita Carillo, that she's fucked every boy in Francisco Javier, and that you're taking her away from me."

Fernando's eyes bored into Memo's at last. "Anita Carillo fucked around?"

"Of course. Why do you think her parents yanked her out of private school? They had to fly her to Miami for an abortion. Oh, she was quite an education. But you wouldn't have wanted her once you got to know her, Fernando, even though you had the hots for her then."

"Not really."

"I know that. You were meant for better things. Look at you! A university professor, a pillar of your community, the head of a beautiful family." He felt Fernando's burning gaze and poured the last of the wine. "I'll protect your family, Fernando. Don't worry. But if you want some practice with that pistol of yours, I can take you out to the firing range at the base. It wouldn't be a bad idea, considering how dangerous this country is getting."

Fernando gave a short laugh. "Memo," he said, "you are such a bastard."

"So I've been told."

15

June 30

"I SAW THAT CREEPY MEXICAN GUY AGAIN," Juanito said. He was pumping hard, tricked out in a snappy cycling outfit, all royal blue spandex and yellow stripes. Félix, in jeans and tee shirt, was glad he was able to keep up even though he was out of training. Shoulder to shoulder they labored up the highway toward the Zeta, their destination the Mirador, five miles and four thousand feet of altitude gain ahead.

"What creepy Mexican guy?" Félix asked.

"I told you about him. He was lurking around in the park in Remedios a couple weeks ago, asking about Don Memo's driver. Didn't they just pull his body out of the Green Lagoon?"

The steepness of the climb gave Félix a moment to pause in his response. All Remedios had been talking about the body found out on the Granados' property, Félix knew. Still, he felt uncomfortable hearing the gossip from Juanito. He wanted to keep that friendship separate from his work out at Sapoclok. Not that Juanito would automatically censure Félix's job; his open mind toward drugs was reassuring to Félix. But still, who knew how far that open mind would take him when faced with the reality of the lab. "The identification isn't official yet," he said. "They're waiting on dental records from Mexico. But poor Uncle Memo, he's upset."

He heard the approaching roar of a truck coming down the mountain and he dropped back behind Juanito into single file as they neared the switchback of the Zeta. The highway was wide enough for opposing traffic to pass comfortably, but truck drivers tended to take up the whole road. Sure enough, before they made the turn, the truck came lumbering around, gears churning, swinging wide and forcing them onto the shoulder. "Fucker!" Juanito yelled after it. After the turn they pulled off the highway under some pine trees to look down at the whole valley spread out below.

"There's Sapoclok," Félix said, pointing out the tiny Pink House under its flamboyant cap of bougainvillea. The Granados property was directly below them, but looked small from this altitude. Even the factory looked unimpressive from here, a low flat roof, a small patch of brown in front. You couldn't tell how tall the chimney was, or see the fence that enclosed the loading dock.

"Where is this Green Lagoon?" Juanito asked.

"You can't see it. It's in the hills behind the house." Félix pointed at the pine-covered hills.

"I see a pond." At the far edge of the hills a piece of green water glimmered.

"That's a different one, over by Buenos Aires. There are like three or four of them, hidden in ravines."

"I remember," Juanito said. "We used to go fishing back in there with your uncles. I just never looked for it from up here."

"We better get going," Félix said, "if we're going to make it to the Mirador and back before it rains." Big puffy cumulous clouds were building over the altipano. They mounted their bikes. An hour later, covered in sweat, they pulled into the Mirador. The overlook, perched at the edge of the

Cuchumatanes, was empty except for its monument, a small step pyramid, and the plaques mounted around it in a ring. Often little kids dashed out from a nearby house to recite the long "Ode to the Cuchumatanes" that was engraved on the plaques. They recited from memory, throwing their arms this way and that. But they'd learned from experience that bicyclists didn't reward them with quetzales the way the tourists did, and stayed away today. The Mirador was windswept and bleak. Beside it the ruins of a glass chalet—built, according to Félix's father, before the war by a general from the capital, who used to visit by helicopter—gave them a place out of the wind to light up the joint Juanito had brought.

"So where did you see this creepy Mexican?" Félix brought the subject up again reluctantly, but he had to know.

"In a bar in Xela where I take tourists, because it has a view of the Central Park. He was at a table drinking with some cops."

"You're sure it was the same guy?"

"Oh yeah. This guy is unmistakable. Unmistakably weird."

"Hmmm." Félix didn't like the sound of it. He should tell Memo.

The rain started lightly as they began the exhilarating glide back down the highway toward Remedios, the mountain face so steep and the valley so far below they could be in an airplane except for the wind whistling against their faces and the raindrops stinging. Faster and faster they dropped in free fall, dodging traffic, breaking only to maintain the fine edge of control, shouting with joy.

The rain persisted all night and the next morning, Sunday, was socked in by rain and fog. Félix got up late. He and Juanito had stayed out late in Huehue the night before, and today Juanito had gone back to Xela. Usually on Sundays the

Granados family went to the Pink House for a barbecue. But with the rain, the river would be impassable and barbecuing unappealing. The door to his parents' bedroom was closed, and he heard their TV on. He guessed they were spending the day in bed. He went downstairs to fix himself some eggs and found Leti with Omar in the kitchen. "Hey," he greeted her. "What's up?"

"I'm babysitting. We're not going out to Sapoclok."

"No duh." Well, he could wait until he was back at work tomorrow to tell Memo about the Mexican.

—

Félix didn't always see Memo in the plant. He arrived Monday morning, punched in his key code, went through the warehouse where there were always a couple of workers stacking barrels or moving cartons around on forklifts, since they did in fact maintain a business in cleaning supplies, which came in and went out in trucks in which the precursors and product could be hidden. In back of the warehouse he keyed himself into the lab, where the assistant he had trained himself after he got back from Mexico was already suited up and preparing the tanks. Félix donned his suit and mask and got to work. Only late in the day, after they'd finished the cook, thoroughly cleaned the lab, and hung up their suits and masks did Memo appear.

"Álvaro," Félix told the assistant, "you can go home. Memo and I have some business to go over."

Memo cocked an eyebrow. "Quite the boss you've become," he said after Álvaro had gone. "You sound like your dad talking to his mozos."

Félix reddened. It was true. Álvaro's grandfather had worked as a laborer on the Granados plantation, back when

Félix's great-grandfather had owned the whole valley and a huge spread up on the altiplano. Even though Álvaro was fifteen years older, Félix unconsciously addressed him with *vos* as if he were a servant. Memo, who came from the lower class himself, noticed such things. "Yes, well…"

But Memo had moved over to inspect the trays of methamphetamine gleaming in the drying racks. "We have a pickup coming tomorrow night. Will this be ready?"

"Yes. We'll bag it tomorrow. We'll have the five hundred pounds we promised."

"That's what I like to hear. Making quotas on schedule. Good work, kid." Memo put his hand on Félix's shoulder. "You've trained your mozo well."

"Look, Uncle, times have changed. Álvaro's making good money."

"And that's what matters. His kids will go to college and be doctors and lawyers, just like yours. Thanks to Eco-Clean!" Memo winked. "We're making democracy happen right here in stodgy old Remedios."

"There's something I'm worried about. Somebody's been looking for Geraldo."

"The whole world is interested in Geraldo now. He's become very popular. Tragedy will do that. It's too bad; he must have gotten involved with some local thugs. I warned him, but he unfortunately didn't listen. It's nothing we have to worry about, Félix. The police will find the guilty parties."

Memo sounded sincere, but Félix still felt uncomfortable and measured his words. "The person I'm talking about could be Mexican, could have been seen in Xela, talking to the police."

"Seen by whom?" Memo was looking at him very steadily.

"A friend."

"Ah, your tour guide friend. The bicyclist. It's good you're getting out, Félix, and engaging in healthy sports. You don't want to spend all your time in the lab and playing video games. Just be a little careful when you go out drinking with your friends. Those barroom confidences can get out of hand."

"Juanito doesn't know anything about what we do here, Uncle. I'll keep it that way." And instead of warning Memo, Félix somehow found himself getting warned.

—

It wasn't drinking that got Félix to lower his guard, or the marijuana which Juanito always provided. It was something altogether unexpected, on a Friday afternoon a few weeks later when he slipped through the back gate into the Pink House, left unlocked for some reason. It wasn't good that the gate was open and Telegram was not in the yard; Félix wondered if the dog had gotten out. He was about to call its name when he saw his mother come out of the bathroom, which opened onto the veranda. She was wrapped in a towel. His mother!

He stiffened, Telegram's name dying on his lips. Her back was to him and she walked away down the veranda toward the front of the house, disappearing from view. He wanted to slink away, through the gate, and back down to the factory, his errand to Memo forgotten. Instead, he crept toward the house, staying hidden behind the kitchen wing. He heard a door slam and muffled voices from inside. Torn between the need to know what they were saying and dread at what he might find out, he worked his way around the outside of the house, past the dining room toward the bedrooms and office, keeping close to the wall, ducking below the high windows.

There had to be an explanation. It couldn't be what it appeared to be. His mother was so modest. He'd never seen her in a towel even in his own house. The brief glimpse he'd had was so unlike her, so loose, so…seductive. He stopped outside the bedroom. The voices he heard through the thick wall were low. He couldn't make out any words. He didn't dare stand up to press his ear against a window. Even though the glass was milky, they might see his silhouette. Frustrated, disgusted, he edged back the way he had come, stepping quietly, feeling a great pressure building inside his chest. He'd gotten back to the kitchen when he heard barking. Telegram!

The dog came bounding across the field toward him, barking furiously. They met at the gate. Telegram jumped on him, tail wagging in greeting. Felix shoved past him, shut the gate, and dashed behind the shed to hide.

"Telegram, here boy!" Memo shouted. Felix heard footsteps approaching down the veranda. "Where were you, rascal?"

"Memo, I have to go. The kids will be waiting." His mother's voice, calm, authoritative.

"Very good, my love." My love? Félix recoiled. He heard Memo fasten the lock on the gate. He heard footsteps receding, doors slamming, a car engine start. He waited until all was quiet to slink back down the hill to the plant.

⏤

Juanito plunked another pitcher of Goat, Xela's signature brand of beer, in front of Félix. How many had they drunk? Félix had lost count. He pulled a roll of quetzales out of his pocket. "Here." He handed them to Juanito. "You keep these. I'm too fucked up."

Friday night in a Xela dive, rockero blasting from the speakers, and the crowd a mix of gringos and locals vying for turns at a worn pool table. "So what's the matter?" Juanito asked. "You look like wolves ate your baby sister."

Félix had come on the bus directly after work, seeking Juanito's company, but not necessarily to talk. He'd mostly been staring gloomily at the pool players. "The cues are crooked. Have you noticed?"

"Yeah. And the table's topography resembles the highlands of Guatemala." He grinned and looked Félix in the eye. "So?"

"What would you do if you found out your mother was fucking around?"

"Oh man. I figured it was something bad. Doña Sandra? She seems so, I don't know, straight and narrow. It's hard to believe. Are you sure?"

"I'm sure. I caught them." Just saying it made Félix feel his gorge rise. He swallowed more beer and clenched his teeth.

Juanito took another sip and swirled his mug thoughtfully. He lowered his voice as much as was possible, and still be heard through the din. "Who is it?"

Félix groaned. "I shouldn't say."

"It's your boss, isn't it? Memo."

Félix didn't answer.

"Holy Mary. That's really fucked up. Does your dad know?"

"How could he!" Félix exploded. "If he knows and lets it go on, what kind of a dick is he?" Félix hunched over the table and lowered his forehead against the rim of his beer mug.

"Maybe there are," Juanito paused, "…extenuating circumstances."

Félix raised his head and laughed without mirth. "Oh, there are. Big extenuating circumstances. The Fuerzas." There it was. Out. He felt relief.

"The cartel? Memo?" Félix heard the confusion and disbelief in Juanito's voice.

"Granados Eco-Clean is a front. We're the biggest meth operation in Guatemala." *We* he'd said, to make it clear. Félix wondered if his words were slurring. This would be the test of how much truth Juanito could take. This was the real deal, not some hypothetical discussion on a mountaintop. "I'm chief chemist."

"Holy shit."

"Yeah. The cartel trained me. University of the Fuerzas is my alma mater. Do you hate me yet?"

Juanito hesitated, maybe buying time to judge him. "What do you do…exactly?"

Félix described the process, using chemical terminology, not wanting to dramatize it, but wanting to impress Juanito. "It's just science. It's easy if you know what you're doing, if you're careful."

"And once you've made the crystal, the…product?" He used the term Félix had used. "Then what?"

"I seal it in plastic bags. It leaves the factory. Memo takes care of distribution. It goes north, out of the country." And to make sure Juanito understood he added, "I've never tried it. I'm not a drug dealer."

"You're dealing with some really dangerous people, I'm guessing."

"You're not kidding. I shouldn't be telling you this. If Memo finds out…" Félix broke off. "I trusted him. Now I want to kill him."

"I don't blame you," Juanito said. "But you can't."

The sound system went dead. They could suddenly hear the babble of voices from the other tables. "Where's the fucking music?" a drunk called out.

The bartender retreated to a PC in the back of the bar and tapped keys until the music roared back to life.

Juanito leaned forward, looking past Félix toward the street door. "Don't turn around."

"What?"

"The Mexican just came in."

16

July 29

MEMO WAS IN HIS OFFICE, staring at the computer screen, deep in thought, when the buzzer sounded, signaling someone at his front gate. He looked at the video display to see who it was. Fuck. Behind the wheel of the Mercedes SUV a floppy hat, thick lips, and eyes hidden behind aviator sunglasses—the Mexican Félix had seen. There was a second man beside the driver, hidden behind the hat. Memo opened a desk drawer pensively, rifled through it for a few things that went into his pockets, and took out his Beretta. He pushed the button to open the gate and walked out onto the veranda with his gun in hand. The Mexican pulled into the yard, killed the motor, got out and stretched, eying Memo without saying anything. His passenger stayed in the car.

"Can I help you?" Memo asked from the veranda, looking down on the man. He didn't raise his gun.

The Mexican took his time. He looked around the yard. Memo felt the disdain emanating from him. No big mansion, no swimming pool, no Thoroughbreds, no outward signs of luxury advertising Memo's power. He glanced at Memo's gun and moved his thick lips as if cutting through sewer sludge. "I think you know why I'm here."

The guy looked like a clown. Memo thought about shooting him and to hell with the consequences. He'd been promised independence and these hovering Mexicans irked him. But the man in the car had a straight line on him and Memo couldn't see what he was doing. "Perhaps you should educate me."

"Your chief chemist has breached security. He has to be removed."

What the fuck. "I don't think that's a good idea. This is Guatemala, not your territory. I have the contacts here. F-40 should have made that clear. The boy is working for me."

"You don't understand." The lips curved. "F-40 isn't in charge any more. The boy has already been taken care of. I have your new chemist in the car. I'm Eduardo Tello. You will have heard of me."

Memo's eyes flickered. "Yes, I've heard of you." The man they called El Bárbaro. He had suspected as much when Félix described him. He was a thug, not a soldier. Without the leadership of military strategists, the brutes were snapping at each other's throats. "What have you done with Félix?"

"We didn't ask you about Geraldo Lopez."

Memo's stomach sank. They wanted him to believe that Félix was dead. He felt a rush to his brain, momentarily clouding his vision. What would he tell Fernando? And Sandra? Something to buy him time to find out what had happened to Félix, if they'd taken him somewhere or...He stared at Tello, keeping his thoughts from showing on his face. His vision cleared.

"This would be a good time to show your chemist the plant," Tello said. "I believe there's a shipment due later this week."

Memo's hand on the Beretta itched. He wanted to use it, wanted to put a bullet right through those stupid lips. Fucked again by Mexicans! Who would undoubtedly like nothing better than to murder him on his own veranda, but were keeping him alive for now, for his connections. How long would that last? He raised the pistol to aim at Tello's chest.

"Raúl, show Señor Galindo your credentials."

The man in the car raised an AK47 trained on Memo.

"Raúl is an excellent chemist and an adequate marksman," Tello explained, as if any explanation were required.

The phone in Memo's pocket rang. Still holding his gun in one hand, he reached for his phone with the other, watching Tello, who said, "Go ahead. Answer it."

It was Álvaro, down in the lab, wondering where Félix was, not like him to be late on a Monday morning. Memo lowered the pistol. "I sent Félix on some personal business," he said into the phone. "He'll be out a week. I'm coming down now with a sub."

They drove to the plant in separate vehicles. An understanding had been reached. No weapons were in evidence when Memo walked the two Mexicans through the warehouse to the hidden door into the lab. Álvaro looked puzzled when Memo introduced him to Raúl. "Don't worry," Memo said. "He knows what he's doing."

Raúl for his part took in the lab with approval. "Small but efficient. You have what we need."

Memo nodded shortly. "There's work to be done. Perhaps we should let these men get to their jobs," he said to Tello.

"I thought I'd stay. I'm interested to see the process."

"Suit yourself. Álvaro, make our guests welcome," Memo said. "Álvaro will get you protective gear. I suggest you wear it. The product is volatile. You'll have to excuse me. I have business to attend to."

Not waiting for the Barbarian's answer, Memo left the lab, letting the door shut behind him with a click of its electronic lock. He greeted the warehouse workers as usual to assure them that all was normal. Asking after their weekends he learned that there had been a baptism; he congratulated the father and went outside. His first step was to get moving, gathering information as he went.

A breach in security. His suspicion went immediately to Juanito. From his car he tried calling Félix. No answer. He called Fernando. "Félix is late for work. Was he out carousing with the chicas last night, or did he go to Xela for the weekend?" He kept his tone light so as not to alarm Fernando.

Sure enough, he'd gone to Xela on Friday and called to say he was staying over. Fernando hadn't seen him since. "What do you think? An accident, or…something else?" Memo could hear Fernando's anxiety.

"Youth! That's what I think. I'll let you know when I hear from him. It won't be long." His direction was set.

Driving south on the Interamericana toward Xela he considered his options. This would be the logical time to cut and run. Now, before Tello suspected he'd do it. It wouldn't be long before the cartel would be finished with him. The network that had taken him years to build with Arcadio, the Pirate down on the coast, Karl in the DEA, a few others, that he kept tight and reliable—would mean nothing to them. They would replace it as they had in Matamoros and Veracruz. Every place they touched would be laid to waste, just as the army had once done. They were the new army, sweeping through the Americas with blind fury. His loyalty would mean nothing. They would kill him.

He kept to the road, his eye on the rear view mirror. He had a roll of hundred dollar bills he'd stashed in his pocket before he'd opened the gate to Tello. It was enough to get him out of the country. He could be at the airport in four hours, or Puerto Barrios in seven. With what he had in the offshore account he could disappear. As he should have years ago in Mexico. He didn't run then because his friends in the cartel had promised him sanctuary, retribution, independence, a fresh start. Now his friends were all dead and the cartel had turned on him. If he made the break now, he could outsmart them and live.

And let Tello win? The fury he'd felt when the Gulf Cartel slaughtered his wife and children boiled up in him again. Let the Barbarian take out Félix, whose loss would devastate his parents? Memo would be responsible. This was not what he had envisioned when he'd involved the Granados family in his business. Could he leave Sandra and Fernando defenseless in the hands of the cartel? He had never expected to feel remorse, not after what had been done to him. Was Félix dead? Damn Tello and the Mexican scum! He had to know what they had done to the boy. He had to shield this family. They were all he had left. He reached Cuatro Caminos, the turnoff for Xela, and turned. There was no escape.

He parked in the center of the city, near the Pasaje Enrique, and entered the shopping arcade, an ornate structure from another century whose pretensions depressed him. Rather than the elegant shops its builders had planned, it housed Internet cafes, cheap bars, and travel agencies appealing to the threadbare tourists who braved Guatemala. Among them he found Trekker Tours in a small alcove adorned with posters of magical lakes, Mayan women weaving gorgeous fabrics, volcanoes and waterfalls. There were two desks. He picked the one where a young woman sat poised behind her computer.

"I wonder if you can help me," he said. "I'm looking for Juanito. He's a guide who works for you."

"You're looking for him, for what purpose?" She didn't seem suspicious yet. Maybe he wanted to book a tour and had heard Juanito was a good guide.

Memo took his time. "I don't want to alarm you. Juanito is not in any trouble." He showed her the DEA badge that Karl had supplied him a while back. "We just need to ask him a few questions. We're concerned for his safety."

The young woman looked at the badge and her brow crinkled. "You're American?"

"No. I'm Guatemalan. Sensitive Investigative Unit." He watched the tug-of-war go on in her thoughts, reflected on her face. She would have no idea what he was talking about, or if such a unit existed, but the badge gave the title weight.

"You'll have to talk to my boss." Her boss had to be summoned from another part of town, so Memo sat in a plastic chair in the Trekker Tours office, watching a young couple pouring over brochures at the desk across from him, asking questions in halting Spanish. From long practice he was able to maintain a calm exterior, not giving in to impatience, not letting the rage and anxiety that simmered inside him show. Finally a tall gringo entered from the arcade. He wore jeans and shaggy hair and was visibly unimpressed by the DEA badge. Memo suggested they go someplace where they could talk in private, and the gringo grudgingly led him to a café next door to the office.

"I'm in the tourism business," he said over coffee. "No drugs. We run a clean business."

"We're not after you or your business, Señor Parker." Memo had his business card in front of him: David Parker, Trekker Tours, Quetzaltenango, Guatemala. "I'm looking for someone Juanito knows, someone who may be in danger. Juanito also may be in danger."

Parker rolled his eyes almost imperceptibly. "OK. I'll call him and you can talk to him." Their table was in the arcade, under the high arched roof, a veritable echo chamber. It wasn't ideal, but Memo nodded, watched Parker tap the contact in his phone, and waited. There was no answer.

"I know it's an imposition," Memo said. "Perhaps you can give me his address. It could be important."

"Oh please! I don't give out the personal information of my employees."

"Normally, that's a good idea. This situation is not normal. Are you familiar with…the Fuerzas?"

"Of course," the gringo answered brusquely.

"Juanito's friend may have crossed them. Inadvertently. Both boys could be in trouble."

"Who is this friend? And how do I know, pardon me, who you are?"

Memo fixed him with a sad look. "Truthfully, the less you know the better. However, if you want to speak to my immediate superior, an American, I can get him on the line." Memo pulled out his phone. Karl would oblige.

Parker held up his hand. "No thanks. I'd rather not. I'm trying to keep a low profile in this country and give tourists a good, healthy time having adventures. No drugs, no law enforcement."

They sat staring at each other for a few minutes. Memo waited. He knew from experience that it was hard to intimidate gringos, who seemed to feel that the laws of nature and other countries did not apply to them. "I'm only concerned about the boys."

Parker rolled his eyes again, more blatantly. "OK. I can get you Juanito's address. But if you fuck with him, I swear to

God I'm going to the embassy, to my fucking congressman." Parker's Spanish was accented, but he had a good command of expletives.

The rooming house wasn't far. Memo went on foot, following the gringo's directions, one long block to the right, two to the left, along narrow cobbled streets that had been laid out in a grid in a time of horse carts and burros—colonial, but not charming in the dying light of afternoon. He walked rapidly to stir his blood. The high altitude cold bit through his light jacket. He should have gone to Puerto Barrios. He could be heading to a Caribbean beach. He found the house, a two-storied cement building with peeling paint, and knocked at its metal door. A tired woman cracked the door open, leaning her mop against the entry wall.

"Seño, good afternoon. Is Juanito in? I'm a friend of his dad."

She looked him up and down and shrugged. "I haven't seen him. He stays out late and leaves early." She opened the door wider to let him pass. "You can look for yourself." She told him where to find Juanito's room on the second floor and continued with her mopping.

The upstairs hallway was dark, lit by a single bulb, and deserted. A knock on Juanito's door elicited no response. Memo tried the knob, and the door opened. He went in and closed the door behind him.

The body hung by the neck from the light fixture in the center of the room. It was naked and covered with gashes crusted in dried blood. The eyes were wide with horror. Layers of duct tape were wound around and around the mouth and jaw—taped shut to suppress the screams, Memo surmised, before they began the beating. Dried blood caked the sides of the head, spilled over the tape and pooled on the floor beneath the feet. Arranged in the center of the dry pool like two flower petals were the boy's ears. *This is what happens to those who hear what they shouldn't.*

The fucking Mexicans. Had Félix, similarly gagged, watched? To get the message that his turn was next? To ponder what would be the torture for the one who talked? Memo looked around the room. Dresser with a TV on top, wooden chair, single bed. Backpack hanging from a nail in the wall. All very orderly. Nothing had been disturbed. He opened the backpack and found Juanito's ID and money, seemingly untouched. The message was the point. The message was for him. He searched the meager room for clues to where they'd gone, knowing he'd find nothing. Knowing where they'd gone: to Remedios, to Sapoclok, to him. He left the room, closing the door behind him, and went downstairs. He told the land-lady nobody was home.

—

Fernando was in his office at the university, still grading tests. His officemate had left for the night. Rain pounded on his window and splashed on the patio outside. A knock came at the door and Memo entered, looking drenched. "I got caught in the downpour," he said.

"I see." Fernando looked around his office for something like a towel, but Memo had already found the Todosantero weaving on top of a bookcase and used it to wipe his face and close-cropped curls.

"I hope you don't mind," Memo apologized.

"No. Sit down." Fernando suppressed his alarm at Memo's desperate appearance. The last time Memo had been in his office was over a year ago. The ronrones had been flying through his window and dashing themselves to death against his walls. If he could turn time back to that day, he would send Memo on his way. *Good to see you, old boy, but I have a meeting, gotta run, let's get together sometime,* and get Memo out of his life. There were no invading beetles now, just Memo's unwanted intrusion. "What's up?"

"I've come from Xela. I tried to call, but you didn't pick up."

Fernando thoughts flashed to Félix. His alarm heightened. He took out his phone and turned it on. "I see you called. So?"

"Félix is fine. Partied too hard this weekend, that's all. He's been working too hard, Fernando. He needs a break."

Memo's tone was meant to inspire confidence, Fernando could tell, but he was not convinced. Rushing off to Xela seemed impulsive for a man as calculating as Memo.

"I gave him a week off, to go adventuring with his pals."

"Pals! What pals?" Fernando felt the words explode out of his mouth. "Memo, what the devil! What the fuck is going on? What have you done with my son?"

"Some tourists he met. They were heading for Lívingston and invited him along. This will be good for him. Believe me."

Believe Memo! "I thought," Fernando said through clenched teeth, "that Félix is indispensible out at the plant. Don't you have a...schedule to meet?"

"No worries. I have a guy filling in for him. Temporarily." Memo was still brushing moisture off his jacket and thighs. He finished and raised his eyes to Fernando's. They exchanged silent stares for a long space. "Just for the week. You have absolutely nothing to worry about."

For this Memo had come to his office at night, in foul weather—to tell him he had no worries?

17

August 3

SANDRA KNELT IN THE EMPTY CHURCH and tried to pray. The Virgin of Remedios looked down from high above the altar, her pure silver robe gleaming in the dim light, her carved face impassive. It was Saturday. Sandra hadn't heard from Félix in a week. He didn't call. He didn't answer his phone. Even if he was on a well-deserved vacation at the beach, as Fernando said, this wasn't like him. When he'd been in Mexico, he'd called her every day. She needed the daily sound of his voice to keep her maternal fears at bay; he knew that. What could be keeping him from calling? She imagined disasters, highway accidents, drowning. Her anxiety mounted each day without him, becoming unbearable, a pressure building in her heart, spreading to her chest, cutting off her breath. There was no relief, not in her routine chores as wife and mother, no solace in her other children, and certainly not in the arms of her lover.

She had stopped seeing Memo. Ever since Fernando had pulled a gun on him and Memo had called to tell her. *Imagine that, your husband tried to kill me.* Mild-mannered Fernando! Memo had chuckled and made light of it. *Show him some sweetness,* he had said, *and it will be all right.* It would not be all right! She'd tried to make things right with Fernando, but she couldn't talk to him about Memo. She tried to go back to what she had been before Memo came between them. It was hard. Impossible. The full magnitude of what she'd done to her marriage stunned her. Her lust had poisoned her family.

Yet, she missed it. Her body cried out for Memo. Just once more, her body begged. A week ago, feeling like an addict, she had sneaked out to the Pink House for one last afternoon. It had felt tainted, felt like a mistake as much as she wanted it. His hands on her breasts, spreading her thighs, had filled her with shame. Coming out of the shower afterward, she'd heard the hounds of hell barking.

Then Félix had disappeared. She was paying for her sins.

A woman came through the cloister door carrying an armload of flowers. Sandra recognized Olga, from the women's auxiliary group Daughters of Santa María, and bowed her head so that Olga wouldn't see her face. Olga passed close on her way to the altar. Sandra burned with humiliation. How had it come to this, that she was afraid to be seen in church praying? Once she'd worn her faith like a badge of honor. How had she gone so wrong? Vanity had been her sin. Her confidence that she was above the laws of man and God. She'd put her pride before her family. Fernando's attempted homicide and Félix disappearance were her fault. God's punishment. She couldn't ask Him for mercy. She couldn't ask the Virgin of Remedios to intercede. For what she'd done there was no cure. She couldn't pray. She waited until Olga's back was turned, arranging the new flowers in the vases on the altar, then got up and left.

From the church she took back streets through town. She walked fast, not seeing where she was, her thoughts racing, trying to outpace her anxiety. Outside of town the sun beat down on her. She was burning up with questions. She needed answers. There was only one place to find them. By the time she reached the river crossing, she'd worked up a sweat. She stopped in the shade to call Memo. "Are you at home? We need to talk."

He was waiting for her on the veranda when the gate slid open to let her through. "Come inside," he said, holding his office door for her. He closed the door behind him and turned toward her. He waited. He seemed calm. That calm that had once soothed her now enraged her. What was it hiding?

"Where is Félix?" she blurted. "Fernando tells me you have some strange Mexicans in the lab. What have you done to my son?" The interrogation came out too fast. She didn't want to accuse him. She wanted to stay in control.

He crinkled his brow, as if debating what to tell her. Which version of untruth, she thought. "I had to send him away," he said, looking into her eyes. "There have been some changes at the top. The new...administration wanted a closer look at our operation. I thought Félix should stay out of the picture while they're here."

"Why doesn't he answer his phone?"

"He didn't take his phone with him. Phones can track a person, you know. He's better off without it. For his sake. For yours." He took a step toward her. She recoiled. She felt his appraisal, a sensitive instrument, gauging her reaction to him.

"So he's in hiding. What have you gotten us into, Memo?" Her voice trembled.

"This will all be over in another week. Félix will be back." He reached out to touch her face. She slapped his hand away.

"How can I believe you? You're a demon!" She backed away from him, toward his desk. Scarcely aware of what she was doing, she picked up an empty glass that was sitting next to his computer. She raised it above her shoulder and hesitated.

"Sandra." His voice was steady, commanding. "Put it down."

She hurled the glass to the floor at his feet, where it shattered against the tiles. They stared at each other in silence. She felt herself breathing hard. He stepped over the broken glass and seized both of her wrists. "I understand," he said. "You're distressed. You have a right. But this isn't helping. Let me take you home to your husband."

She stood in silent fury, resisting his grasp with clenched fists. His eyes advertised love and sympathy but guarded the unknown. She felt overwhelmed. She gradually slumped and dropped her hands; he let them go. "Very well. You can take me home." She straightened her shoulders. "But you'd better get my son back to me."

Or what, she wondered. What power did she have over him? The power to come into his bed again? She allowed his hand to steady her arm when she climbed into his car, allowed his respectful kiss on her cheek at her door, as if to prove to any watching eyes that all was well between them, that between Memo and the Granados family there were no hidden strains about to rupture. "I'll keep you informed," he said. "Try not to worry. Reassure Fernando." He drove away as she fitted her key into the door.

That night, alone in bed with Fernando with the light still on, she said, "I'm very afraid, my love. I saw Memo today. I think we're in trouble."

Fernando tensed beside her. "What were you doing with Memo?"

"Trying to get some answers. Memo has Félix hidden somewhere, away from the cartel. I think the cartel has turned on him."

"That's it! I'm going to call your father. It's time for a raid on that plant. A military SWAT team with help from the DEA.

We need to get these criminals out of our lives while there's still time. Your father will take care of the bastards." How desperate Fernando had to be to think that her father, her puny, upright father, could save them from the forces of the cartel as well as the law.

"What about Félix? What if the cartel has Félix? We can't attack them. We can't endanger Félix." *More than they already had*, she thought, by sending him to Mexico, embroiling him in Memo's business.

The silence stretched between them like an abyss. Sandra felt their helplessness. Finally Fernando said, "I'm going to Memo in the morning. He'll take me to Félix or I'll go to the police. I started this, Sandra. I'm going to finish it." Fernando sounded brave. Certain. She didn't know where his certainty came from. "Are you with me?"

She shivered. "Yes."

"Good." He switched off the light and turned his back to her. She pressed against him for warmth, or hope, she wasn't sure which. He reached for her hand and drew her arm around him. "We're getting through this, Sandra," he said into the dark. "We're finding Félix."

She tried to pray. *I don't deserve your mercy, O Lord, but I beg you. I'll do anything to get my son back.*

—

Although he'd promised Sandra to have a showdown with Memo the next day, they'd both forgotten in the anxiety of the moment about the christening party for Fernando's newest great-niece that Sunday. The entire Granados family gathered at Georgina Springs to sit around long tables set out under the trees in the park. Fernando and Sandra kept their trouble to themselves and pretended to celebrate while the adults feasted and the younger children ran around the islands in the springs and bounced on suspension footbridges. By the time they returned home after the party they were as tired and wrung out as if they'd been the ones running and bouncing.

It wasn't until Monday morning that Fernando stood at the gate of the Pink House pressing the buzzer over and over. Buzzing and buzzing. Telegram leapt at the gate barking, but Memo didn't appear. He hadn't answered his phone either. His ire rising, Fernando got back into the Toyota that he'd picked up earlier from the shop, finally repaired six weeks after the accident with the bus. He drove the short distance to the plant and parked in front of its shuttered loading dock. This time when he buzzed, the door opened. It was opened by the Mexican, the one Memo told him was called Eduardo Tello, the one he had seen with Juanito on the morning before the accident. He wasn't wearing the floppy hat and aviator sunglasses now, but he still looked odd, with his pale, shoulder length hair. Memo hadn't volunteered any more information other than Tello's name and that he wouldn't be staying long; Fernando wasn't to worry. Memo's favorite refrain.

"Where's Memo?" Fernando demanded.

"Memo isn't here. But you may come in."

Perhaps Fernando should have been put off by the weirdness of Tello at the door, or warned by some survivor instinct that this wasn't safe. But what could be safe, after all, at this late stage? Tello radiated hostility. Fernando should have felt threatened. Instead, he relied on the adrenaline of rage. He'd been pushed around too long. This was his property, where the Mexican had no right to be. He forced his way past Tello, striding in with false bravado. Inside, the warehouse looked no different than it had on his earlier visits. Workers moved among the aisles, loading and unloading sacks and canisters onto hand trucks, oblivious to their contents which were, he'd been assured, what they purported to be: cleaning supplies. Tello moved easily through the aisles, leading him toward the back. They reached the door to the lab. Tello turned and his lips curved in a smile. He punched a code into the lock. "After you," he said, holding the door open.

The menace was blatant. Fernando's rage sputtered. Was there a way to back out? Two men in white coveralls looked up from the control panels in front of the giant steel cauldrons of the lab. Their faces were obscured by hoods and masks. There was no way Fernando could bolt. With a sense of doom, he stepped inside. Tello closed the door with a resounding click. "You may sit," he said, gesturing toward two metal folding chairs.

"Who the hell are you to tell me what to do on my own property!" Fernando blustered. "Get Memo in here."

"Memo will not be returning. Matamoros hasn't been satisfied with his performance. We're taking over."

"The hell you are!" Fernando felt trapped, desperate, afraid, enraged by his fear. "I'm calling the police right now." He grabbed the phone out of his pocket, switched it on, and stared at its screen as if it were a portal to safety.

"Your phone has no signal in here." Fernando looked up from his phone to see that Tello now had a gun trained on him. "Also, the door can't be opened from the outside. And no one in the warehouse can hear anything from inside this room. One thing Memo did well was the construction of this lab."

The two men in coveralls stood frozen. "Get back to work," Tello told them. "We'll watch." The gun nudged Fernando toward one of the folding chairs. Tello sat in the other.

Fernando collapsed into the chair, his knees feeling weak, his breath short, his heart palpitating as if on the verge of infarction. The two men flipped switches and turned dials. Fernando heard hissing, and the largest tank began to burble. A sharp smell filled the room. Fernando watched anxiously for signs of escaping gas or liquid. Tello watched him, seeming amused.

"It's your business," Tello said. "You haven't seen a cook?"

Fernando bit back a hundred questions. What had they done with Memo? With Félix? Why weren't he and Tello wearing protective gear? Tello slouched back in his chair and crossed his legs, the gun now dangling in his relaxed hand. The men in coveralls darted from gauge to gauge, adjusting dials. Fernando waited, expecting an explosion any second.

"We want your cooperation to keep the business running smoothly." Tello's voice startled him.

"The business is all in Memo's hands. I can't help you." He steeled his voice.

"Was. Now it's in our hands. We don't want any interference from you, or the police." Tello stood up suddenly. "Álvaro! Come over here." One of the covered figures moved away from the bank of controls and hesitated. "Raúl can take care of it."

The small man shuffled toward them. Fernando could see his face now through the mask, a man he had known since boyhood. They had to be nearly the same age, but Álvaro's face was weathered and creased from years of working in the sun, and now wrinkled with fear. He sat stiffly in the chair that Tello had vacated.

"From now on there will only be our people in the lab." Tello pressed the barrel of the gun against Álvaro's chest, cloaked in the coverall, and fired. The shot reverberated through the lab like the explosion Fernando had been

anticipating and he jumped in his chair. Álvaro made a strangled sound and slumped to his side, sliding out of the chair
onto the floor where he lay on his back, his arms and legs
convulsing. Fernando watched transfixed while red erupted
across the front of the coverall and blood pooled like molten
lava on the floor, Álvaro gurgling and struggling for breath.
Fernando could see his face through the mask, contorted in
a grimace of agony. Tello stepped back to avoid the blood.
Raúl continued working at the dials. To Fernando the minutes seemed to stretch into an eternity, with the gunshot still
echoing in his brain and Álvaro writhing at his feet, the pool
of blood growing, turning dark. Finally Álvaro's eyes rolled
back in his head and his twitching started to slow. Fernando
felt warmth in his crotch, and realized he'd pissed himself.

"I'm not shooting you," Tello told him. "As I said, I want
your cooperation." He slid the gun into some recess inside his
jacket and withdrew his phone. "If you disobey, your punishment will be harsher than a bullet to the heart." He swiped
his thumb across the phone's screen several times, then held
it out for Fernando to see.

Still dizzy with shock, it took Fernando some time to
focus on the photo in the small screen, a face. His son's face.
Félix's eyes and mouth wide open in a silent scream. The base
of his neck, where it should have met his torso, ripped open
in a bloody stump.

"What! . . ." Fernando lunged forward toward the phone,
screaming. Tello yanked it back and shoved Fernando back
into the chair.

"You have three more children," Tello said. "And a wife.
You must be very careful this doesn't happen to them. Very
very careful."

18

SANDRA WAS LOOKING OVER Leti's math homework when Fernando pulled into the driveway and parked. She and Leti both watched him from across the patio. He got out of his car without looking their way and went directly upstairs. "Papá got the Toyota back," Leti observed.

"Yes. It's fixed. The shop called early this morning," Sandra said, biting her lips. The hours had passed with no word from Fernando. What had happened when he confronted Memo? She couldn't imagine it. Could Memo have agreed to take him to Félix? Or at least to reveal where Félix was? He'd been gone so long! Why hadn't he called? He seemed to be avoiding her. She wanted to follow him upstairs. She looked back down at the page on the table. "Look, Leti, at this problem: $3x - 4 = 5$. Solve for x. What do you have to do first?"

Leti moaned. In her first year of middle school, her teacher had just introduced a unit on algebra. Sandra had liked algebra, the beauty of balancing equations. The problem seemed so simple to her, but Leti clearly wasn't ready for it. Sandra fought back her impatience with the teacher, with Leti, with Fernando. The lesson in equations was still plodding on, multiplying and dividing with random sprinklings of letters and numbers, when Fernando came back downstairs, showered and changed. This time he came over and gave them both a kiss on the cheek. "I'll be late," he told Sandra. "Meetings tonight after class."

She looked into his eyes and tried to penetrate his thoughts. Fernando turned away quickly and left. Sandra gazed after him, screaming inside.

"Mamá?" Leti's voice brought her back. "Are you worried about Félix?" Her daughter was so attuned to her moods, it startled her. Sometimes Sandra believed Leti could read her mind. It was the result no doubt of their being the only women in an all-male household. Leti imitated Sandra, asked Sandra's opinion in all things, and looked up to her. But what had made her think of Félix?

"No, my love. Why should I be?"

"Maybe something happened to him."

Why wasn't she a better liar? Why had she told Leti that Félix hadn't called? "He's fine, having fun with his friends."

"Wasn't he supposed to be back from the beach by now?"

"No. At the end of this week. Now let's finish this last problem."

"Mamá? Félix says I should go to college, like Aunt Carolina did." Maybe it was the algebra that made Leti think of college. It was such a grownup subject, not useful for buying and selling and making change, the normal uses for mathematics that Leti saw around her every day. College in Leti's imagination would be difficult and abstract.

"Of course you'll go to college, my love." Leti, despite her struggle with algebra, was Sandra's brightest child and worked hard in school.

"I'd like to be a lawyer like Aunt Carolina. But…"

"But what, sweetie?"

"Then I couldn't have a husband."

Sandra's heart sank. Leti knew that her mother had quit college to marry her father. She took Leti's hand. "You can do both, mija. Don't sell yourself short."

"Did you sell yourself short, Mamá?"

"A little." Sandra smiled weakly. "But times have changed." She heard Omar's cry from his room. She kissed Leti's hand and stood up. "The baby's awake." He wasn't really a baby any more, but he still took an afternoon nap, providing Sandra with precious time alone with Leti while Walter was at soccer practice. "Finish your homework and we'll go out for ice cream."

They walked together to the new restaurant on the park, Omar between Sandra and Leti, each holding his hand. Leti was almost as tall as Sandra now. Sandra stole glances at her daughter. Quiet and responsible, she would be a good mother someday. Was she bold enough to be a lawyer? She wasn't flamboyant like Carolina, but there were different types of lawyers, Sandra knew. Rather than loud and combative, Leti would be the diligent, dependable one that you relied on in times of trouble. She was that to Sandra already.

They were seated at a wooden table in the bright front room of El Rincón, Omar happily patting his strawberry ice cream with a spoon, when the man at the table next to theirs stood up and left. Leti's eyes widened and she brought her hand to her mouth. "Mamá!" she whispered, staring at the vacated table.

"For heaven's sake…" Sandra was about to chastise her daughter for being nosey, when she saw what the man had left behind—a newspaper open on a headline. "Execution in Xela."

Sandra reached out and plucked up the paper. The photograph under the headline showed a figure hanging by the neck, dead. "My God!"

"It's Juanito," Leti said. "I thought he went to the beach with Félix." Her eyes filled with tears.

"No!" Sandra said quickly, scanning the paper. "It's not Juanito. It looks like him, but it's not Juanito." She folded the newspaper and stuffed it into her bag under the table. "Watch out! Omar's ice cream is about to hit your sleeve."

Leti grabbed Omar's hand. "Come on, baby. Be a good boy and eat your ice cream."

"You eat!" he protested. Leti let him guide the spoon to her mouth and she took a bite.

"See? Yum! But I have my own." She dug into her sundae, eyeing her mother as she did. "Aren't you going to read the article?"

"I checked the names. It's not him," Sandra repeated. "Don't think about it." She blew on her cappuccino. She felt faint. Again she felt Leti detect her lie. *Juan Carlos Maldenado Cruz* and *gangland style murder* were as far as she had gotten before panic seized her and triggered her reflexes to hide the newspaper. She reeled with the implications. Juanito murdered. Before her worries had been vague. *Dead* had never been spoken in her thoughts, although it lurked just behind them. Was Félix dead too? But it couldn't be! Memo couldn't have kept that from her. Fernando couldn't!

She would read the article later, when she was alone, and search it for mention of Félix, any connection to the Granados family and the lab. Leti couldn't know. As long as she could protect Leti, then it wouldn't be true. She returned to their earlier conversation, like a moon circling a planet, unable to escape. "Félix will be home for Walter's game next Saturday. He promised."

Leti looked at her evenly. "Certainly, Mamá." She dipped her napkin in her water glass and started cleaning Omar's face and hands. As if Leti knew that her mother's sanity depended on her.

~

Driving away from the plant that morning with his pee-soaked pants sticking to his thighs, Fernando's thoughts reeled. He couldn't tell Sandra what he'd seen in Tello's phone. How could he possibly tell her?—*Our son is dead.* He wouldn't even know how to form the words. He barely saw the road in front of him. When he got to the turn toward home, he turned the other way and headed up toward the altiplano. He didn't know where he was going. He drove up the steep face of the Cuchumatanes with buses coming at him around blind curves.

He hadn't been so scared since his night in the woods with Pepe. He'd pissed his pants that night, too. Then he'd been just a kid, his life ahead of him. For all his fear that night, things had turned out well. He'd resumed his life, finished school, gone to college. The Violence had ended. He'd become a professor, married, brought children into the world. A whole good life had still been ahead of him the night the safe house burned.

What was ahead of him now? Success, prosperity, grand-children—everything he'd counted on was lost to him. Everything he'd built would be destroyed by Memo and the cartel. No really, when he was honest with himself, by his own actions. How could he have brought this on his family? What could he do to save them? Scenarios played out in his imagination. He would send Sandra and the children away. He would sacrifice himself to the cartel, let them run their fucking operation and be their front. But where would Sandra go? Where was safety? Not Mexico, although that was where they had family and connections. The cartel was there.

The US? What would Sandra do there, scrub toilets? And how would he get her there? The cartel had taken over the coyote trade. No longer could you trust neighbors and cousins to guide you on the perilous journey al Norte. The cartel had infiltrated the country, infecting every village and person it touched. Tello was in his body eating his organs and replacing them with monstrous tumors. Fernando felt himself a dead man.

Another scenario came to him, of strapping himself with explosives and walking into the plant, right up to Tello and pulling the cord. Could he do it? Where would he find the expertise and the materials? Would he have the nerve?

He hadn't even been able to shoot Memo.

Memo! Now there was a guy who could blow up Tello, and probably wanted to. Where the hell was he? Was he dead? Tello was cold-blooded, but there was no evidence that he was a match for Memo's icy intelligence. Fernando would bet that Memo had gotten out alive. He wished he'd searched the Pink House for clues.

He'd reached the top of the altiplano and was crossing its broad expanse. Empty fields stretched out on either side of the two-lane, bordered by stone fences and spiked hedges of maguey. A harsh and forbidding landscape sprinkled with lonely houses. A sign announced the turnoff to the Blue Unicorn. He turned.

Long ago his brother Pepe had brought him and Memo out this way. It was before Memo had met Anita Carillo, and the two of them had been innocent boys just having fun. The excursion with Pepe had taken them to an abandoned hacienda that seventy years earlier had been the center of a vast holding of horses and sheep owned by a rich Spaniard. Fernando's grandfather had been foreman on the ranch. Pepe had gone there as a boy on horseback with his grandfather, after the Spaniard had left and the hacienda was shuttered. Pepe had told Fernando and Memo tales from its glory days while he showed them around the outbuildings. He had a key to the foreman's snug little cabin nestled in a stand of pines behind the hacienda. "This is where I'd come if I ever had to hide out," Pepe had said that day.

Of course, when the Violence came, Pepe had fled to Mexico. The altiplano hadn't been far enough. Fernando wondered if Memo remembered the place. He followed the road, still a rough dirt track, avoiding potholes and boulders, worried about bursting a tire, for what seemed like a very long time. Maybe he'd remembered the wrong road. But finally he came to it, off to the right. He pulled into the yard, parked, and got out. The hacienda looked shabbier and more forlorn than he remembered. The wind howled across the altiplano. No one was around. He circled around back to the foreman's cabin. It looked as abandoned as the rest of the place, the padlock on its door rusty. His foolish hopes died, he slammed his car door, and despair seized him once more.

Driving on past the hacienda he came to the Blue Unicorn. He'd seen ads for it on TV. Out in the middle of nowhere a crazy Frenchwoman had built a dude ranch with stables for her Quarter Horses and a small guesthouse. She organized multi-day trips on horseback for exclusive clientele. Fernando had never met her, but he was desperate. He drove past her No Trespassing signs and stopped in front of the guesthouse. Dogs barking at her side, she marched toward him from the stable. He recognized her from the ads. He rolled down his window but didn't get out of the car. The pee on his pants had dried but he felt unclean.

"Can I help you?" she demanded, signaling to her dogs to sit.

"I was driving by and thought I'd stop in to inquire about availability. Friends coming from the capital tomorrow, horse enthusiasts, are dying to visit the famous Blue Unicorn. Do you have anyone staying with you now?"

"You didn't think of calling first?"

"I wanted to see your place before recommending it to my friends."

"We're closed, as the sign on the gate said. The gate that you drove around to get in. Our reservoir has dried up and we're building a new one."

"Yes. Sorry about that. My friends will be so disappointed. I...was hoping to persuade you...but I won't bother you any longer." He rolled up his window. She stood between her dogs, her arms folded across her chest, as he started his engine, turned around, and drove away, humiliated.

Out of ideas, even desperate ones, he drove home, arriving in midafternoon. He slunk past Sandra and Leti on the patio, went upstairs to drop his pants in the hamper and shower. He couldn't wash away the image of his son's bloodied head in Tello's cellphone. Telling Sandra he'd be late, he left the house again and drove toward Huehue.

He didn't know how he would teach. His mind was coming apart. He was stuck at a light when his phone rang. He looked at caller ID. Don Alejandro. The police! His other option: turning himself in, letting the authorities take over, letting them raid. Fear and relief washed over him. Sandra's objection had been for Félix's safety. That no longer held. Tears sprang to his eyes. He answered the phone, not knowing what he would say but wanting to hear his father-in-law's voice.

"Have you seen today's paper?" Alejandro asked. "Juanito Maldonado was executed in Xela."

Fernando felt it like a blow to his solar plexus. Another execution. How many more? When would they come for the rest of his family? "Don Alejandro, can I talk to you? Not at the station. Some place private."

"I'm at home. Come out to the house."

He called the secretary at the university and told her his classes for the day were canceled. When he arrived at his father-in-law's he steeled himself for probing questions and disapproval, but Alejandro was cordial, not suspecting, Fernando knew, the full horror in store. "Doña Lidia is out," Alejandro said. "The servant girl is home with a sick child. We're alone." He ushered Fernando into the dining room. Papers lay scattered on the table along with a copy of the *Prensa Libre* folded open to the regional news. Fernando sat down and stared grimly at the headline and photo.

"We don't know much more than what's in the paper," Alejandro said. "The body was there several days before the landlady discovered it. I don't know what's wrong with her olfactory. Xela's cold, but it must have stunk. We think it's drug related. Probably the Fuerzas. Félix has been involved with this kid." He stopped and stared at Fernando with a worried expression.

Fernando bowed his head and flicked a finger to the inner corner of one eye, where he felt tears. "Félix is dead, and it's my fault." He choked the words out with difficulty.

"What?! I don't believe it!" Alejandro shot up from his chair and stood looking down on Fernando, pressing against the table with his knuckles, his arms stiff.

Fernando broke into unrestrained sobs, his shoulders shaking, tears coursing down his face. Alejandro groaned and sat back down, his face crumpling. Fernando felt his appalled stare but couldn't stop the convulsive weeping. Alejandro watched, stricken but dry-eyed, as if waiting to be convinced of the dire news. Finally he handed Fernando a handkerchief.

"When you can pull yourself together, you'd better tell me about it."

Fernando's crying subsided. He mopped the tears and snot and haltingly began the tale, starting with the Rattlesnake. Alejandro moaned at intervals—"How could you have been so stupid?" "I trusted my daughter to you!"—but mostly encouraged him to talk. The unburdening felt painful to Fernando but necessary, like vomiting. Alejandro slowed him down and asked questions about the details of the meth lab and its layout, taking notes and drawing a sketch on his pad, getting Fernando to correct the sketch. Finally they got to the culminating point of Fernando's horrendous tale. "The photo of Félix on his phone, are you sure it was authentic?" his father-in-law asked.

"There was no mistaking it. Tello showed me three shots. Before…and after."

"Could you tell where they were taken?"

Fernando shook his head. "In some woods. No way to identify them."

"Hmmm. I'll look into it. Try to get more information."

Fernando, feeling hollowed out as if his guts had been scraped clean, said, "I'll do anything. I'll go to prison. Anything to get the cartel out of our lives."

"It won't be easy," Alejandro said acidly. "We can raid the lab. I'll start setting it up right away, but it will take time. Meanwhile you must behave to the cartel as if you've told no one. You have to keep Sandra in the dark. We will have to get her and the children away. But you stay here. You've mixed yourself and all of us up with these killers and now you're going to have to tough it out. As God is my witness, Fernando, for once in your life you've got to have some balls!"

19

THE SUN WAS RISING over the eastern horizon when Memo left the hotel grounds and strode across the black sand toward the breaking surf. At dinner the night before he'd been warned not to swim in the ocean today. The beach of Monterrico was notorious for its undertow and drownings, and the riptide would be particularly fierce for the next few days. But Memo had swum in far more dangerous waters. He dropped his towel on the black sand and dove into the surf. A few strong strokes took him out beyond the breakers, where he rolled onto his back to gaze up at the lightening sky.

He should have left Guatemala days ago, when the photos showed up in his phone. Tello had won. Even knowing it was coming, the shock had sickened Memo. Soon Fernando and Sandra would find out Félix was dead. They would blame him. He'd thought he was numb to loss, but blamed himself. His life in Remedios had ended in disaster. He had to flee. He'd left the Pink House with his bankroll, his weapons and essential papers, and driven straight to Monterrico as if hellhounds were snapping at his heels. He'd checked in under a false name, using a US passport, one of several passports he had for emergencies. He had no doubt that the cartel could find him here, although he'd destroyed his phones and computer and every possible device that could track him. They would expect him to be in Grand Cayman by now. But he wouldn't be going to

Grand Cayman; he could access that account from anywhere. There were places he could go so remote and undesirable not even the cartel would bother coming for him. Meanwhile he was dawdling in Monterrico, for one long last look at his native sky, while rocking on the bosom of the Pacific.

He bobbed in the warm water, washing away rage and grief. It had been foolish to give his heart to the needy boy, to the boyhood friend, to the impetuous woman. Ah, Sandra! Poor suffering Sandra. He wouldn't make that mistake again. He was emptied of human emotions and desires; he was an animal on the run. Like an animal he would survive. He felt suspended—between the life he'd lost and a new one that held no appeal. The thought of starting over exhausted him. He almost drifted off to sleep. When he roused himself to see where he was, the tide had swept him far out from shore. The palm trees lining the beach were tiny. The empty sea stretched southward 12,000 kilometers to Antarctica, with not a rock or bit of land to cling to. He shook away his reverie and began his workout, swimming hard. An hour later he walked onto the hotel grounds, flushed with endorphins, his towel around his shoulders, sweat and salt water dripping off him. A waiter came out of the dining pavilion to intercept him. "There's a message for you at Reception," he said. It was the job of the resort staff to know all the guests, not difficult in a small facility.

Memo raised a questioning eyebrow. "I doubt that, but I'll check."

A stone path led past the pools, palm-shaded lawns, and circle of thatch-roofed bungalows to the reception building. It was still early on a weekday morning and few guests were up. The receptionist who'd taken the call told him, "That was all he said, Señor Gomez. 'Call your uncle.'"

"It must be for a different Gomez," Memo said. "I don't have an uncle."

Back in his bungalow, which despite its rustic exterior was sleekly appointed and air conditioned, he powered on his new phone, a cheap "bean" as the drug runners called it—throwaway and untraceable. He called Karl, his DEA connection. Uncle Sam; they'd laughed when they'd dubbed him that. Trust Karl to track him down. He waited through many rings.

"Your nephew here. What is it?" he asked when Karl picked up.

"Huehue police are ordering a raid on your plant. DEA and the military to cooperate."

Good old Karl, still reliable. Maybe this was the unfinished business that had kept him in Guatemala, destruction of the evil he'd brought down on the Granados family. He repressed a reflexive desire to call Sandra, to tell her that General Arellano would protect her and Fernando. It was past the point where he could offer them comfort. With him gone, maybe they could find solace in each other. "Go ahead," he told Karl. "You have my blessing."

~

For Fernando the week crawled. After baring his soul to Don Alejandro he went to a bar, not his usual modus operandi. It was a place where no one knew him. Even so, he felt raw, exposed, watched by unseen eyes as he nursed a drink. But better than facing Sandra with her probing questions, her unspoken accusations. When he got home late Monday the household was asleep, but Sandra was waiting up for him in an agitated state. She thrust the newspaper article about Juanito at him. "What did Memo say about *this*?"

"He's on top of it." Fernando had thought his story through, rehearsed it in his mind so that he could deliver it without breaking down. "He's gone to Matamoros, to straighten things out with the cartel. He left this morning. When he comes back he'll bring Félix." He could barely speak his son's name, for fear she would detect his lie.

"Where is Félix?"

"I...don't know, Sandra." He forced himself to look her in the eye as he lied, when what he wanted to do was cover his face and weep. He'd never done anything so difficult. She stared at him, impatient, demanding.

"And who is running the lab?" She wouldn't flinch.

"Two Mexicans the cartel sent. A chemist and some other guy."

"Who are these people, Fernando? On our property, in our lives! A boy is dead; he was Félix's friend, a good boy. Our son is missing. And you're telling me Memo has run off?" She was starting to sound hysterical. He felt himself coming apart and was relieved to hear the flushing of a toilet and the slamming of a door.

"We have to be quiet. We'll wake the kids. It will be all right," he said. He didn't add *Trust me*.

Three days followed, hours and minutes ticking slowly, sluggish yet explosive with tension. In the mornings he left for the university, hoping a return to his routine could alleviate his misery at least for the hour he taught a class. But he could hardly focus on what he was saying or what was being said to him. All he could see was his son's face in Tello's phone; all he could hear was Tello's refrain, *You have other children*. At lunch Sandra put food in front of him and he felt nausea. He had to force himself to eat. After his evening class midweek, he stopped by the police station to see Don Alejandro. He didn't dare use his phone. Even walking into the station house felt risky. Could the cartel be watching him? Still, he couldn't bear waiting. He found his father-in-law behind a desk. "What are you doing here, Fernando?" the small man demanded.

"Any progress on the, uh, plant? When do you expect—"

"You know I don't discuss police business!" Don Alejandro cut him off, his eyes darting around the room where police officers sat at metal desks. Fernando realized he'd become the center of attention. "This department is under intense scrutiny since the Salcajá massacre. We'll get those narco bastards along with every corrupt officer in Huehuetenango."

Even here Fernando wasn't safe. Even here, his father-in-law was telling him, the cartel had ears. The next morning he drove to Don Alejandro's house before class. The older man was a little more open with him. "Do you know how many officers were removed from the PNC last year? Two hundred nationwide! You think that's solved the corruption problem in the police force? Hah! Now every officer in Huehue is suspected of drug ties. In this environment I have to arrange a raid on your plant. It will happen, I swear before the Maker of the Universe. But I'm negotiating with three bureaucracies—police, military, DEA—to get helicopters and forces, and trying to keep it secret from my own men. Next week at the earliest."

Fernando didn't think his organism could stand another week of such agony.

"Get Sandra away from here this weekend," Don Alejandro added.

How, without telling her the truth? Fernando went home in the evening. He spoke to his children, watched the news with his brothers, bore Sandra's anxiety, hiding his terrible knowledge. He held up. It wasn't heroism; he wasn't a heroic man. It was necessity. Lives depended on his performance. If Tello caught wind of the raid it would be the end of it. That night in their bedroom he tried to sound as if all would come out well. "Sandra, we need to get away."

"Get away? From what? What's wrong?"

"All this tension. It's not going to bring Félix home any faster." For this lie, he knew she would never forgive him. "Let's go to San Cristóbal this weekend. We haven't seen Emilia and Delfino since your father's birthday party."

Quick jaunts to see his sister and her husband were normal. He could plant the idea of the trip and then back out at the last moment, sending her and the children without him.

"Are you kidding? Or is something going on you haven't told me about? Walter has a game on Saturday. Have you forgotten?"

"Right. Of course. It was a dumb idea." He sighed and turned out the light. "I'm tired." Another failure.

Friday morning he heard screaming coming from the kitchen, a long penetrating howl that built and built, sounding very like an approaching siren, only it was human. He jumped up from his desk and rushed to the kitchen doorway. Sandra stood there, clinging to the counter and wailing until she ran out of breath. She gasped for more air that seemed only to fuel the wail that started up again. He saw a cutting board and knife and some vegetables, but didn't see any blood. It sounded as if she'd cut off her whole hand. "What is it? For God's sake, Sandra!"

She pointed to the floor and continued wailing. Her phone lay on the tiles. Fernando picked it up and looked at the screen. It was the photo of Félix's bloody head. His stomach lurched and he stuffed the phone in his pocket, took hold of Sandra and pulled her against him. "Stop! Before the neighbors hear you!"

Already Omar appeared in the doorway. He'd been watching TV. Fernando put his hand on the back of Sandra's head and pressed it against his shoulder to muffle the scream. It stopped, and she convulsed into sobbing. "Mami cut herself, that's all, Omar. She's going to be OK."

He dragged her to the sink, turned on the tap full blast, and stuck her hand into the water. Sandra leaned over the sink as if she would vomit into it. Her body hid her bloodless hand from view. Tona ran toward the kitchen from the back of the house where she'd been hanging laundry. Fernando wrapped Sandra's hand in a dishtowel and steered her toward the two onlookers. "It's a bad cut. I'm going to take her to the doctor. Tona will take care of you, mijo; finish your program. I'll be back soon."

He hurried Sandra past them, got her to his car, and pushed her into the passenger seat. She slumped forward against the dashboard, resting her head on folded arms, still crying. The dishtowel remained wrapped around the uninjured hand. "Tona, get the gate!"

He pulled out of the patio and drove away from the house, turning on the main street away from town. Sandra continued her hysterical crying, jangling his nerves, tearing into his soul. He passed the turnoff to Sapoclok and continued up toward the altiplano until finally he found a place where he could pull over, out of sight and earshot of houses. He stopped the car and turned toward Sandra. "Please my darling…stop crying if you can…for just a minute."

Her crying shuddered to a halt and she raised her head from the dashboard to look at him with bloated red eyes.

"Is Félix really dead?" she asked.

His world collapsed. He couldn't keep it from her any longer. "Yes. I'm sorry. Oh God, I'm sorry." There wasn't anything else he could say.

"You knew this! What you told me about Memo was a lie. You've been lying all along! What's the truth?"

"Memo has disappeared. I went to your father. I confessed everything…the cartel, the lab, everything I've done. He's planning a police raid on the plant."

"I don't believe this. You're a monster! I want to die." Her hair was a mess and her face wet with tears.

"You can't. For the children's sake. You have to take them to San Cristóbal." He picked up the dishtowel that had dropped onto the floor and held it awkwardly. "Let me wipe your face. You have to stay calm. Go to Emilia's house in San Cristóbal. Tonight. Tell the kids…" What could they tell the kids? That Walter had to miss his game. That their lives were in danger. "That it's about Félix. Break it to them slowly, up there. Let me deal with the cartel."

She snatched the towel. "You! What can you do against the cartel?" She wrung the towel between two hands but didn't dry her face.

The barb struck home. Tello had sent the photo to Sandra. He wasn't content to threaten just Fernando. He had no limits. "Tello will be watching us. I'm the decoy. So they don't suspect the raid." Did he believe this? Or was he afraid to leave, afraid that if he tried to flee with his family Tello would go after them. He clung to the hope that if he stayed he would keep Tello's focus on him long enough for his family to escape.

"What will happen to you?"

Hadn't she just called him a monster? "Does it matter? Do you care?"

A heavy silence fell between them. Finally Sandra broke it. "Oh, Fernando. We've both made so many mistakes. Not just you. I don't think our punishment will ever end."

They looked at each other. "I'm sorry," Fernando said. "I wish..." He choked with the enormity of all he wished. He couldn't finish. He couldn't tell Sandra that he loved her, that this would all be fixed somehow, that they would recover. On the way back into town he stopped at a pharmacy and picked up supplies to bandage Sandra's finger. As if her howling that morning could have been caused by anything so inconsequential. But he wanted desperately to preserve the innocence of his youngest child.

20

"COME TO THE PLANT RIGHT AWAY," the voice on the phone demanded.

"Who is this?" Fernando looked at the clock by his bed. Seven thirty. Light streamed through the cracks in the closed shutters. He'd overslept. He'd been up past midnight waiting for Sandra's call. She'd made it to San Cristóbal, accompanied by his brother Edgar, the steady one. Hearing her voice on the phone, Fernando could at last rest.

Only to be startled awake by the phone again. "You know who it is, Señor Granados. Your presence is required immediately. Don't make me come get you."

Fernando felt his bowels loosen. "What do you want? I teach a class at the university in an hour."

"No phone calls. No side trips. Do you think your wife and children are safe in *Mexico*?"

A fresh stab of fear. Fernando knew what the cartel was capable of. He dressed quickly, buttoning his shirt with trembling fingers. He slipped his pistol into his pocket. He didn't know what good it would do him.

Where should he go? Directly to the police. To Don Alejandro. He could be at the station in twenty minutes. Mobilize them for an immediate attack. Hope the cartel's ears were not on duty.

What did Tello want? *No side trips.* Did the cartel have people in San Cristóbal right now? Undoubtedly they did.

Fernando could call Elena, tell them to get out. And go where? Where could they hide? *No phone calls.* If he went to Tello now, sacrificed himself, was there a chance he could save Sandra? He pulled his car out of the drive and headed toward the Sapoclok. It felt like his fate.

Was it his imagination, or was there a faint miasma of toxic fumes hanging over Granados Eco-Clean? A truck was backed up to the loading dock. Workers loading barrels looked up at him briefly, then continued with what they were doing. Their presence was strangely heartening. Whatever Tello was planning, there would be witnesses. He stepped up to the small door beside the loading bay. The eye of a camera peered out at him. He rang the buzzer and waited.

The door opened, and Tello, clothed in a hooded coverall with its protective mask shoved back on his head, pointed a gun at him. "Come in," he said, "The gun is going into my pocket, so as not to alarm the workers. It will still be aimed at you."

Fernando's brief surge of courage sank. He walked through the warehouse passing local peasants he knew, recognizing among them Tona's husband. Tello followed close behind him. They entered the glowing white light of the lab. Inside the lab the Mexican chemist stood at a bank of switches. Chemicals bubbled inside the glass domes and through the tubes connecting the row of cauldrons. Tello closed the door to the warehouse with an ominous click. "Raúl, come here a moment," he said, lowering his mask to protect his face but not moving the gun that was trained on Fernando. "Search him."

Raúl removed his rubber gloves and patted Fernando's jacket, pulling out the pistol, which Tello took. "Were you planning on using this?" he asked derisively. He didn't wait for Fernando's answer. "You've been very stupid. I need you alive for now. Otherwise you wouldn't be. Sit down."

Once again Fernando found himself sitting in the lab. Álvaro's blood was cleaned up, but its memory was vivid. He couldn't speak. Raúl went back to the dials. Tello sat in the chair next to Fernando. Tello rested his gun on his knee, which twitched up and down. "How much longer, Raúl?" He sounded restless. The two Mexicans were swathed in their protective gear. Fernando felt naked and helpless with the chemicals percolating around him. His fear bubbled with the tanks.

"An hour until filtration. We can rush the cooling."

"The precursor will be finished loading into trucks in a few hours." Tello addressed Fernando, "By the time your friends in the police get here, we'll be long gone. I hear there's a back road into the mountains that avoids police checkpoints. Do you know the road?"

Did it matter what his answer was? Would Tello shoot him if he said the wrong thing? As if in answer to his unspoken question, Tello said, "You're coming with us. You and the workers. If we run into any police you'll be our human shields, for what you're worth."

"You're taking the workers with you?" Fernando thought about Tona's family, the other families he knew, simple local people. "What will you do with them?"

"We're relocating." Tello shrugged. "Perhaps they'll find employment in our new venue."

Were they all slotted for death? Had he brought disaster not only on his family, but on his whole community? "Why did you send that photo to my wife?"

"You disobeyed me. I don't like disobedience. You're going to get to watch what I do to your family."

Fernando fought back tears. The gun continued to bob up and down on Tello's twitching knee. If this were a TV drama Fernando would snatch the gun and turn it on the Mexicans. He'd drive them out into the warehouse where the workers would witness his heroism. He would hear helicopters, and soldiers in riot gear would burst through the door. The movement of the gun mesmerized him. He tried to imagine the feeling of his arm darting toward it, the strength of his hand grasping it. He glanced up at Tello's face behind its mask, the thick lips pursed. "This place stinks," Tello said. "Did you fart? Or worse?"

There was that sharp smell in the lab again. The tubes connecting the tanks gurgled. Fernando's vision swam with tears he couldn't stop. Faint rattling came from the shelves in the corner containing bottles and flasks. The gun bounced on Tello's knee. The rattling got louder. All three men turned to stare at the shelves. The gun stopped bouncing and Tello raised it and aimed it at Fernando. "What's that?" Tello said.

Fernando's chair vibrated. The vibrations spread to the tubes between the tanks, to the tanks themselves. "Raúl! What the fuck!" Tello said sharply.

The rattling increased in volume. The vibration became more pronounced and climbed to the ductwork overhead, the drying racks, even the metal roof. The roof clanged, the ductwork drummed, bottles crashed from the shelves, the noise swelled to a deafening roar. Fernando felt the floor shudder and roll under his feet like ocean waves.

"Shit!" Tello screamed.

Raúl made a lunge for the nearest cauldron that was swaying on its stand. "We have to get out of here!" he shouted.

Tello staggered toward the door and fell. The gun flew out of his hand and spun across the floor. Fernando watched the row of domed cauldrons bob and sway like drunkards on a spree. His heart raced and he felt a terror so sublime he mistook it for exhilaration. *This is it!* he thought. He dove toward the spinning gun. He thought of salvation. He thought of helicopters and rescue and Sandra and the kids safe in San Cristóbal. His fingers closed around the gun like a lifeline. From the floor he saw the cauldrons bobbing and swaying. One by one they toppled over and smashed on the undulating floor, enveloping him in a blast of light and heat and sound.

21

2014

SPRING IN ASTORIA, QUEENS, USA, is a miracle of rebirth, particularly to a person from the tropics who has never before experienced such a transformation. A person who arrived in NYC in the dead of winter, when snow was piled in blackened mounds on street corners and in parking lots and lay in treacherous glittering drifts in parks. When bare and lifeless trees looked like they would never recover from the shock of the frigid air, air that bites the skin and burns the lungs of a person from the tropics with savage ferocity. Particularly when that person is a bicycle messenger who every day must ride from Astoria, Queens, into Manhattan, braving the icy streets and snowmelt lakes and sucking the cold air into his gasping lungs.

Spring comes and the air turns gentle and fragrant with blossoms that erupt in great balls of pleasant color on every bush and tree. A person from the tropics, where blooming is scattered throughout the year and muted by ever-living foliage, has never experienced such intensity. Félix had experienced other sorts of intensity—of hatred, fear, and loneliness—since he'd escaped by rolling out of the back of Tello's car as it sped over the mountainous highway at night, escaping with cuts and bruises but no broken bones, but with the never-to-be-forgotten trauma of his friend's ghastly death dogging him as he fled, through the underbrush, over the mountains, into Mexico, for all the months of his arduous journey al Norte. Now, riding home from Manhattan, he allowed himself to feel a little hope. He rode up the tree-lined street to a two-story brick row house occupied by four Guatemalan families, where he had a small room in the basement.

He left his bike in the foyer, which was crowded with baby strollers and shopping carts and boots left over from winter and let himself into his landlady's apartment on the first floor. "Is anybody home?" he called, practicing his English.

"In here, Felix." He liked his name pronounced in American: *Feelix*. Passing through the living room with its mattresses neatly lined up on the floor and its beige couch and end tables stacked with folded clothes, he found his landlady's daughter Jennifer sitting at the kitchen table, her laptop surrounded by an array of open books. "Nutrition paper due tomorrow. I'm gonna be up all night."

In her first year at LaGuardia Community College, Jennifer had been born in America, spoke native English and was teaching him some, although he was bad at it. Switching into Spanish she said, "Mami left beans and tortillas on the stove. Help yourself."

Her parents had started out by allowing him to keep food in the fridge and graduated to letting him chip in for groceries. Scooping beans onto a plate, he sat down next to Jennifer, enjoying the unaccustomed pleasure of being alone with her. "Where is everybody?" he asked.

"Friday night treat. They took the whole gang out to McDonalds." Jennifer's cousins, aunt, and uncle were packed into the front of the apartment. It was a temporary arrangement; they'd arrived two months ago, not long after Félix had found his way to Jennifer's mother through connections he met on the road. Doña Rosa had a soft spot for the unlucky. Jennifer tut-tutted. "That's what my paper's about. Fast food, obesity, diabetes; my mother should read it." Jennifer aspired to be a nurse.

"Your mother's not fat," Félix objected.

"She has a body mass index of 26.4. Technically she's overweight."

"What's your body mass index?" Félix sopped up the bean juice with his tortilla.

"I'm not telling you!" She tossed her long black ponytail. "Technically, it's normal."

"I'd say it's technically perfect." She had small round breasts, a narrow waist, and wide hips, revealed by her tight tee shirt and jeans. That wasn't everything he liked about her, but it didn't hurt.

"You're full of yourself tonight." But she sparkled at his compliment.

"I'm getting my ID tonight."

"From that cook at Taverna? Beware of Greeks bearing gifts."

Félix's second job was washing dishes at the restaurant. Minos would give him dinner, but he preferred Doña Rosa's home cooking. "It's not a gift. I paid for it. At least now I won't have to be scared of cops."

"Felix, this is America. You're brown. You'll always have to be scared of cops. You think a phony driver's license is going to change that?"

Actually, his skin was nearly white and his dark hair was wavy, not gleaming and Indian straight like Jennifer's. Nonetheless, he knew what she meant; he looked Hispanic. "You'll just have to marry me and make me an American," he said.

"In your dreams! I'm not screwing up my career by getting married."

"Hey! Just a joke." At least half a joke. "You'll marry a gringo doctor and never have to go back to Guatemala again." She'd complained about their triennial trips to visit her grandparents in a backward village in Quiche. When she was ten, she'd told him, her father had made her wear traje, the native outfit of their village, while they were there. By the time she was fifteen she'd flat-out refused. It wasn't "home" to her, even if her accent was pure chapino.

"You poor baby. You miss Guatemala. You deny it, but I know you do." She picked up one of her books and started flipping through it. Félix stood up.

"I've got to go to work." He washed his plate and fork and put them in the dish drainer. "Good luck on your paper. If you get an A we'll celebrate. I'll take you to McDonalds." She threw a pencil at him as he left the room.

He'd never told her why he left. Or how his fears of American cops were nothing compared to the terror that had driven him north. Félix would never go back to Guatemala. Late that night he came home from the restaurant to his room in the basement guarding the card that would keep him in America—his photo, a name, a birthdate, a number. He was tired, but he opened his phone to Facebook, where he lurked but never posted, to his mother's page. His mother had moved with her remaining children back into her parents' house. He knew she thought that he was dead. He'd seen the anguished postings by his brother and sister. His mother's face looked out of the photo on his screen at him. Her face tugged at the deepest part of him. He wanted to call her, yearned to hear her voice, to dry her tears, to tell her he would come back some day after he'd made good in America. (Maybe he would go to college, become a real chemist!) But he remembered her betrayal and his heart turned to stone. He came from a place— Jennifer, with a sneer of derision, would call it a culture of *machismo*—where a woman's sins can't be forgiven. To forgive her would be to forgive himself, and that he couldn't do. He would never forget Juanito's screams. Juanito had died because of him. Because Félix, like his mother, had loved Memo. He'd seen no mention of Memo in his forays on Facebook. He was glad the man had disappeared; he wanted to forget him. He knew that his father had died in the earthquake that had destroyed the lab. His poor father, who only ever wanted to do his best for the family. His family was destroyed, he had no friends in Guatemala, and he would never go back. He slid his mother's face from view.

Acknowledgements

FOR THIS, MY THIRD BOOK SET IN GUATEMALA, I am most grateful for the support, guidance, love, and advice from my friends in Guatemala, which I consider to be my second home. For their privacy's sake I'm not naming names, but they know who they are.

This is a work of fiction. There is no town called Remedios in Guatemala. The Virgin of Los Remedios plays a small role in the Spanish conquest of Mexico, but she is overshadowed the appearance of the dark-skinned Virgin of Guadalupe. In Guatemala City there is an image of Our Lady of Remedies that dates from earliest colonial times in a church of the same name, in a country where you will find Mary in many of her roles as the universal mother: Our Lady of Mercy, Our Lady of Candelaria, Our Lady of the Conception, Our Lady of Expectation, and the image on the cover of this book, Our Lady of Sorrows. I think of her as a cultural rather than a religious image, in a country that reveres all its mothers.

The Fuerzas is also a fictional name, and the events in this novel never happened to any of the people who inspired my characters. However, I researched actual events in many journalistic sources, including but not limited to: "The Untouchable Narco-State" by Frank Smyth in *The Texas Observer*, 2005; "Zetas in Guatemala" by Paloa Hurtado in *El Periódico* of Guatemala, 2011; the Report of the Global

Commission on Drug Policy, June 2011; "Here's what 'Breaking Bad' gets right, and wrong, about the meth business" by Dylan Matthews in his *Washington Post* blog; and many articles in *The Washington Times, Los Angeles Times, New York Times, Latin American Herald Tribune, Prensa Libre* and *Plaza Pública* of Guatemala, *The Tico Times* of Costa Rica; and the important blogs *Insight Crime* and *Borderland Beat*.

I am less interested in reporting on the big picture of drug trafficking in Guatemala and more interested in the inner lives of my characters. And so, for their help in keeping my characters real, many thanks go to 100 Monkeys, my writing group of more than fifteen years: Michael Buening, Judy Chicurel, Rita Hickey, Mary McGrail, Susan Miller, Laura Reissman, Lauren Sanders, Nancy Weber, and Iromie Weeramantry. Special thanks as well to my wonderful editor, Victoria Scott.